Herald
Unexpected

Herald Unexpected

Volume I of the Tapestry's War

MAC TOIRNEACH

XULON PRESS

Xulon Press
2301 Lucien Way #415
Maitland, FL 32751
407.339.4217
www.xulonpress.com

Paperback ISBN-13: 978-1-6628-3171-3
Ebook ISBN-13: 978-1-6628-3172-0

I dedicate this story to the memory and feeling of the lady who urged me to start writing. Wherever she is, whatever she is doing, I pray she finds peace and calm without me.

Finishing this story is built upon my Christian faith and the hope of finding my future wife, whoever she will be.

TABLE OF CONTENTS

Quadrant One:

Strange Things Happen When Looking for Coffee

Written by Mac Toirneach

No one ever achieved great things without risk. You may fall down after trying, but what's worse is to never try. Take on your challenge with a practical sense of logic, but quail not in fear of it, for that is the deadliest weakness.

— Jii Reshiik, a 4ᵗʰ rank Geipul, on his gloriously celebrated victories in war.

F irst, dear audience, a warning about the loveliness of being crazy. This story is told by an unreliable narrator, which means Oruaural will say *many* things. There are also many things Oruaural will *not* say, like how Oruaural loves to speak about themselves in the third person. Of course, I *can* speak in first person, but I love speaking in third person even more! Oruaural will also take this opportunity to mention something *important*. Ahem... *hoom hoom...*

The nexus of thought will mix with the nexus of emotion. The Shifting Stones will be shattered, divided, warring against themselves and face their *greatest* foe. Realize thy strength is found in completing the union — question it not. The battle will destroy. The dead will live. Justice will win the day. Thy herald is the man unexpected even of himself, unknown to Aerth.

Understandably, you may not understand that. Even if it was more direct than other stories. This story was never meant to be one of those anyway. My author puts his words together differently than others because admirable as other authors may be, different is better than everything being the same. Everything being the same is **boring!** There is **nothing** worse than... that blah feeling, because it is empty of happiness and all the other things that are wonderful in life. If the prophecy has intrigued you, then you will understand better by continuing as Oruaural's audience. The *Prognostication of the Golden Transmogrification* refers to strangely ambiguous things from another universe, as prophecies often do. Naturally, you're free to disagree. If you are entertained in the course of this story, that's **good** – you can enjoy it all the better. However, Oruaural won't hold it against you if you do *not* enjoy this story. That is a matter of personal taste, beholden to your natural reaction.

You shouldn't worry about Oruaural's boisterously playful half replacing your clothes with sheets of beef. At least... not *again*. The prank backfired anyway. There are still many things on Earth Oruaural doesn't understand and probably never will.

One important aspect of the *Prognostication of the Golden Transmogrification* means I must achieve my goals within the prophecy, hence a specific quality to certain plans. This also means that Oruaural needs someone to help you make sense of this story. Because if it's not obvious enough already, Oruaural doesn't have all their marbles, although that's also an ironic joke, since Oruaural is wealthier than you might imagine. Hee-hee!

Oruaural understands that some may consider Oruaural's understanding as... haphazard. But Oruaural understands this much, most stories have a beginning, middle, and an end. Though sometimes not even the storyteller knows where their account fits in. Some stories are so complicated, that complete descriptions are impossible, even with firsthand experience. Some storytellers may even go insane. But every story starts somewhere. This one begins with a dream my author had. Being mortal, he couldn't pinpoint exactly what it meant to him, but it has been a strong influence on his longing for love and companionship. What he didn't know was how the dream related to individuals from alternate universes.

In this dream, the character Ernest wandered through an unfamiliar open area and saw bricks. Lots of bricks. Bricks in every direction. The location looked like the Broadspace–downtown Boston's public square—an open clearing with low, circular walls, all made of bricks. Some things were the same; some were completely different. He saw a bronze chessboard with a few pieces embedded in the concrete. The concrete columns weren't styled to resemble thick tree trunks as Ernest remembered, but as tall Greek or Roman plinths. The statue of the spinning ballerina was replaced by another unfamiliar one, a-

Ernest's attention focused suddenly on two people, to the exclusion of the milling crowd —a man and a woman. Although the man looked exactly like Ernest, he was sure he wasn't seeing himself. The man was thin, strong, with bright red hair. He strode over the bricks in what seemed like a calm, relaxed gait, walking toward the circular walls. Then he noticed the woman and smiled, walking faster.

The woman's dark hair flowed in shining waves to her shoulders. She looked preoccupied with a book until realizing the man was interested in her. They greeted as if they recognized each other and discussed going into a nearby bistro. This wasn't the popular "Cake n' Coffee" chain; this had the serene face of a crowned maiden for the logo. The name was altered, too. It was-

Suddenly, Ernest was inside, pleased to see the two people enjoying their time together.

Then the dream faded, and time marched rapidly on. Ernest felt like he met that woman from the dream years later, but not at a bistro. Instead, this meeting was at a fast-food restaurant. *That* story is for later. Most of you already know what Earth is, for general description. Because you have never lived in the world of Aerth, this description is the greater challenge. First of all—the name. Are you wondering how to pronounce it? Why? You already know how. Think of the word 'aerospace' but instead of 'space' say the 'th' sound. Push your tongue against your teeth! Do it now! It's so fun!

There are five different *sapient* races in Aerth. Since sapience refers to the thinking mind, while sentience refers to the awareness. Your thermostat is "aware" of the temperature, but doesn't think about it. To understand what Aerthlings are, try imagining anthropomorphized animals that can understand complex issues and solve problems logically. Perhaps even "furries," if you like. However, they all wear clothing as normal people do. (Did you think they'd go without? Come on, this story is family friendly! Or at least PG-rated.) Alternate universes differ from yours, but morality is universal. Clothing is important for its functional purposes to protect against the weather, for personal expression, and allows the wearer a certain amount of privacy in public. Clothing encourages a wholesome respect for other people, guiding others to look for the attractive qualities in a person that go *beyond* the body, like humbleness, intellect, gentleness, and common sense. Love. Ambition to succeed and achieve good purpose. These things are hidden in the heart and mind, not the body. The more the body becomes the focus, the less of those other qualities are noticed. Which is sad, because the body is meant to be a sacred vessel for the heart and mind. It might surprise you how closely people here share this belief, despite how much their bodies differ from humans.

Now, you need descriptions of the five distinct races of Aerth. Each have average sizes similar to that of humans: the Vungir, the Thvenel, the Quastrans, the Tasdo, and the Aejlii.

Though human sized, Vungir appear related to bats and can fly. Whether living in simple homesteads or large cities, they prefer cave-like homes, either natural or carved from a deep vertical hole. The homesteads' entry shafts branch into furnished rooms which are guarded above by a fortified wall. Entire cities may be dug underground this way, but mountains are preferred. The upper levels almost always house the richer neighborhoods, the middle class are in the middle levels, and the deeper levels are slums. Each level has benefits and problems. There is some conflict, but every sizable Vungir settlement has its ironshirt guards to keep the peace.

Also able to fly, the Thvenel are similar to human-sized wasps. Their communities are made largely of paper combined with adobe mud, like wasp nests, but are reinforced by wooden beams. The walls and fortifications of the Thvenel communities reflect the aggressive, warlike culture of their ancestors. Inside, are apartments or offices made with uniformly shaped and sized rooms. Regimented by zoning laws, there are multiroom sectioned units or single-cell units, but all are residential and commercial—except for the royalty. Not all the Thvenel communities are ruled by royalty now. Many of the monarchies were subsumed into the Grefarn Empire, a dictatorship with iron-fisted plans to rule the world. There are still some Thvenel monarchs holding onto their regions, but they are a small number, waging desperately vicious wars on their respective fronts.

Quastrans appear inspired by the form of a ball-shaped, three-legged and three-armed crab. Preferring to build with stone or lumber, often using pieces larger than they are, the Quastrans create sprawling structures above and below ground. They feel most comfortable living on coastal land but will tolerate the discomfort of cold or dry climates if necessary. Their strength, together with a thickly plated, spiky exoskeleton, encourages many into careers of construction or as heavy ground troop mercenaries. Quastrans love bright colors, so their cities favor shades of yellow, red, orange, green, and light blue. Though they can breathe underwater, Quastrans walk awkwardly in water and cannot swim.

The Tasdo culture thrives on trade and merchant exchanges. Being half-snake, half-humanoid, they adapt their homes to the land, sometimes building partially submerged in the ground, above ground, or even in the treetops. They use a wide variety of building materials, having no style they cling to, using the best of whatever's available. Tasdo communities reflect their adaptability, not just in their architecture, but also to whatever culture is more dominant in their region. Despite their reptilian appearance, they are *not* cold-blooded. Sort of. Their diet metabolizes sugars and carbohydrates into methane. They have a system akin to Earth's electric eel, which provides an internal spark, and the gas burns against a special heat-conductive tissue network, distributing the temperature.

Last on Oruaural's brief tour among the people of Aerth are the Aejlii. Like the Quastrans, Aejlii are amphibious. Unlike Quastrans, they are excellent swimmers, with both feline and fish features. There exist no better, faster, or more spry sailors in all of Aerth! For this reason, nearly every oceangoing shipper relies on Aejlii navigators, channel/harbor pilots, or at least hires them as deckhands. With no large cities, many are content to live in simple hunter-gatherer villages spread throughout the shallows of Aerth's tropical seas. These small Aejlii villages among the coastal seafloor habitat derive their tools mostly from materials found in the oceans. Their culture relies on clan family lineages, whereby influential households or tribes control entire villages, depending on the size of the tribe or village. Not all Aejlii live without refined technology. Some are cosmopolitan enough to seek education about their world, and one village even operates its own shipping line.

That should help you understand the basics of Aerth's societal structure. Brief though it is, a summary of how these people live, helps to describe who they are. A nice bonus with this summarized description, is that it allows Oruaural to pick and choose *how* to describe it. A final note. Though all of Aerth's societies are in their medieval period, the advancement of technology and innovation remains hidden—guarded against those who would misuse that innovation—for the sake of the innocent. This is what you're enjoying as Oruaural's audience—the challenge for the heroes to not just prove themselves honorable, but to stand defiant against the *dis*honorable.

Greatness doesn't seek to prove itself; it *is* the achievement. If more people realized this, fewer would be disappointed. Fewer excuses and—

"The audience may be confused about me interjecting here, but I think they might've been wondering if you're going off on a lark in the narrative. We should probably get back to the story."

"Of course!" The Oruaurals laugh. "This particular part of the story is about recruiting you as the story's scribe. Yes! Oruaural *likes* it! Come on Ernie, you shouldn't blush; it's nothing you need to be embarrassed over. As you said, our audience is probably confused about who's speaking. So it's a *perfect* opportunity to introduce you."

Oruaural suddenly turns towards the audience. "Oruaural apologizes if this seems out of order, but you simply *must* meet Ernest Redsmith! Though your closest word in this situation is scribe or stenographer. The one whose job is to actually write down as close as possible (at least comprehensively), the verbatim of what Oruaural describes for their story. Oruaural has heard of a job called an amanuensis, which may be more accurate, but most people aren't familiar with it. Perhaps Oruaural should also introduce *themself!* I'm using first person to introduce myself, though as you may have noticed, I prefer third person. Be grateful I'm not trying one/quarter-th person to narrate, or even 1,148,067[th] person! I am Oruaural, mad mighty administrator of the Shifting Stones. I commissioned Ernest to take narrative dictation of my experiences in this story. I could have tried writing it myself, but I get easily distracted, and how could Ernest introduce me? He is not me—I am! Sorry if breaking the fourth wall feels weird, but we needed introductions. What method is more amusing or direct than this? If you're not sure how to have a conversation with a fictional character, you don't have to answer."

Turning back to address Ernest, the Oruaurals insisted "Don't omit that—you're being introduced, silly. Most authors don't use the idea of their own characters dictating to them. We need to know who is whom, and what is what, even if this method may be unintentionally confusing. Keep in mind, dear audience, that although

I dictate, I don't refer to an iron-fisted meanie lording over the backs of their people. Well, now that previous sentence did, but—"

Ernest speaks up again. "Oruaural... back to the story?"

Oruaural seemed to think for a moment. "Yes, Oruaural will get to it. Oruaural wanted to quickly begin describing Oruaural's realm and the adventure in Aerth, but a proper introduction means Oruaural must introduce Ernest's background! It must be specified that *Oruaural* wasn't meeting Ernest, but *Ernest* was meeting Oruaural! Anyway, start with the argument you were having with Jeannette on the phone. You did start this largely because of her."

As Oruaural pointed out, Ernest was recruited into transcribing this story. The recruitment was a *strange* series of events. Like many humans, he studied diligently in high school, then pursued various jobs after graduation. Ernest had always struggled with social awkwardness and finding love, despite a desire for a fulfilling marriage.

Maybe this is why he had a peculiar, perhaps unhealthy, fixation on a dream he experienced some years ago. Already described earlier, the dream may be purely a metaphor—the visual representation of love and unfulfilled life. Its symbolism is vital to understanding Ernest's feelings.

The longing for success in work and love and a lack of fulfillment seemed inescapable to Ernest. When the breakup with Jeannette happened, he felt almost felt like he should have expected it. Afterward, his life was hopeless, without meaning or purpose, and he began to spiral into depression. This story is about how those dark thoughts changed for a better direction in one of the craziest ways possible. Because evil can't plan or prepare to fight a crazy *and* strategic strength. Especially if Oruaural is *crazy like a* fox...

Jeannette and Ernest were talking over the phone.

"Ernest," Jeannette said, sounding annoyed, "Vegas is a big city, and I don't feel comfortable about it. I like the idea of a vacation, and that I could visit my cousin after she's been in prison, but..."

She trailed off, so Ernest knew what was coming was uncomfortable for her. "But what?"

"Well," she said hesitantly, "Vegas is such a big city. I don't know how safe I'd feel, especially with my son along."

"Come on," Ernest insisted. "Do you know how many millions of tourists visit it every year, many from the other side of the globe? Do you think *they're* fearful? Boston is a big city too, and I lived there for about six years! I know what to expect."

"Yeah, but you didn't have to move far from Veil—it's just across the river—and, um..."

"Jeannette," Ernest reminded her, "I lived on Bourke Street. *Bourke.* I've told you before how awful that neighborhood was. Nearly every week, some idiot—often the same person—would ask me if I was "looking." At first, I genuinely didn't know they were talking about drugs, but then the grimy appearances they had, their glazed eyes, and I realized they were feeding their own addictions. I had to ride my bicycle past the aftermath of a shooting! The police were all still there, interviewing witnesses!"

"Yeah, but..."

"What? I don't understand why you suddenly want to call off the vacation when—"

"Look, I didn't want to say it, but I don't trust you."

"'D-don't trust me?'" Gasping, Ernest dropped his hand, nearly dropping the phone too. Shaking, he put it back to his ear. "Why on Earth not?"

Trying to justify her answer, Jeannette said. "In almost all the time I've known you, I've never seen you take a leading role in our relationship. I need a strong, confident man, someone who is firm about what he wants, what he does. I've seen you back down more than I'd like. You'll probably always be worthless, never with any money to support us, unable to be a *real* provider. I—"

"You told me when we started dating, you didn't want me to be controlling! Because of that, I've always worried I'm being too heavy-handed!"

"Well," Jeannette countered, "I feel like you were always more feckless than controlling. I wanted someone to lead in unfamiliar areas of life, and you were never that man."

Struggling to keep his anger from devolving into crying, Ernest yelled into the phone "You wanted me to take control but to not be controlling! That makes **no** sense!"

"It makes all the sense in the world!" Jeannette screamed. "You behave like an immature child, as if you're retarded! Grow up!"

"*Me?*" Ernest retorted. "You're the one who was a drunk for three out of the five years we dated! You're the one who threw temper tantrums, like that time at the *Milk Maid* diner when the poor clerk ended up with your sundae on her uniform. Did you forget you threw your tequila ice at your young son? I'm sure you don't want me to remind you when you spiked my coffee with that powdered 'sweetener.' You knew what that stuff was, but you still did it, and just before church service, too!"

"Oh, there you go again, trying to put all the blame on me. Ugh, I'm tired of trying to explain. Goodbye."

"No, wait!" Ernest cried.

But Jeannette had already hung up.

He fumed, of course, but Ernest also didn't want to feel like he had wasted all his time with her. He wanted to say that even if she did need a leader, he couldn't guide do that, if half the time she didn't want it. That if she really wanted the idyllic dream of a family she'd told him about in the beginning, then she had to dedicate her commitment to it. He hoped she would call back.

Ernest waited out the next week, hoping Jeannette wouldn't throw away the last five years of time and emotional effort. But by the week's end, there was no sign of reconciliation. Ernest was alone... *again.* He realized he shouldn't have expected commitment from her. Ultimately, she didn't expect commitment herself. The news headlines, as awful as they usually were, held little interest to him now, even news stories he would normally get *very* emotional about.

Night after night, Jeannette invaded his dreams, reminding him of the good times they'd had together. As if he could ever go back to her, or somehow reach for a life with someone who wasn't reaching with him. If that was even possible now, it would probably require an alternate universe, to make a new start where their mistakes never happened. While the dreams of his past with Jeannette were warm and happy, waking up alone was harshly cold. It was as if he had a longing to go back and recapture that life. This must've been why he kept finding himself in that first date. That dream was always the most clear and realistic.

"Ernest?" Jeannette waved at him. "Earth to Ernest? Have you decided yet?"

Ernest and Jeannette were on their first date at *Quesa Mesa*, a fast food diner favoring low-cost Mexican food. It was a popular nationwide chain, the name of which roughly translated to "cheese mountain." He could never seem to remember what happened before the dream's events, only that he remembered it was their first date.

"What?"

Jeannette rolled her eyes in annoyance. "What's your choice from the menu?"

"What were we doing before?"

"Oh, come on." She punched playfully at his arm. "Quit fooling around and pick something."

Although Ernest could never recall how they set up their date, he always remembered a general idea of what led to it. Almost ten years after high school graduation, he had started wondering about the class reunion and found a link. Interestingly, only two other members of his graduating class were listed. One had no contact info beyond a name; the other had a profile on a social network—Jeannette. Ernest asked her about the reunion, mostly in the interest of catching up on what happened after school, but also in the hope that he could conquer his loneliness and be happy. Chatting became friend requests and following each other online. Ernest hoped he wouldn't seem like a creep, so he tried following at a distance. After a few years, Jeannette surprised him by suggesting a date. Her young son would come along so she could look after him.

He told Jeannette where to meet him and to look for a redhead wearing an emerald-green shirt and blue trousers. They hadn't studied in the same class but rode on the same bus during their senior year. Ernest often spent the rides home gazing out the windows or working on schoolwork. Distracted as was by the scenery passing outside the windows, or solving his math problems in the bus seat, he didn't know Jeannette had developed a crush on him. When Ernest incidentally found her profile on the class reunion website, it felt all the more amusing how she was also riding the school bus with him. She told him her classes at the VITOC were to become a dental hygienist, while he sought a career in engineering.

Ernest was confused but happy that Jeannette seemed to like him right away. Unsure if he was being pushy, Ernest offered to play one of his DVD movies and cook lasagna dinner. As a pleasant surprise, Jeannette accepted for the evening and the comedy movie was nice. So it was, that after the night shrouded the sky, the movie and dinner finished, Jeannette left with her young Joshua. Ernest waved to them from his apartment's door, and all had gladness in their hearts.

But always to wake up alone. An awful dread filled Ernest that he would never enjoy the pride and happiness of being a husband or a parent. Never to have his own family and experience that gladness. Was it all an unrealistic dream? The idea that Jeannette believed a happy family was only fantasy gnawed at him. Surely, he wouldn't despair forever. The situation had to improve. Right?

Jeannette's feelings had always been fickle, which tortured Ernest, as if his soul was being ripped asunder every time she changed her mind. During the relationship, he wanted to scream at her to love him or leave him, but for God's sake to make a choice and stick with it. He thought about taking the government-subsidized antidepressants, but they were addictive. Though he was depressed, he didn't want a dependency. When Ernest tried reaching out for her help, Jeannette responded with foul language and insults. The vehemence of her anger made her seem like a completely different woman. Though he was still tortured by his dreams, he knew now he had to stay away. She was a stranger to him. He wanted to let go but didn't know how. After five years, she was the closest he had gotten to the blissful hope of married life.

The breakup occurred around Christmas. While so many others were smiling and enjoying the cheerful season, Ernest was miserable. He spent an entire week purging his life of her reminders—pictures, gifts, clothes, old cards, even online posts about how wonderful it all used to be. Consumed with a roiling mix of feelings just beneath the surface of his behavior, he alternated between wanting to sob, or scream in a raging fury. The rising divorce rate mentioned on TV felt like a cynical commentary from society. He was not a violent person, but he almost felt like one— at least temporarily. One of those people who cracked and went on a rampage. Looking back, he was horrified at how close he might have come to a psychotic break. Though cliché, Jeannette felt like the literal woman of his dreams. Since he could actually visit the place from his dream, next to one of the popular *Cake 'n Coffee* bistros, Ernest wondered if it was prescient of his future. Jeannette was so close to that idealized figure he wondered if the dream was a prediction of her.

Ernest sought the help of a good therapist and volunteered at church, which helped him keep calm and carry on. However, the more he thought about it, the more he wondered if the situation was for the best. Jeannette had made it *absolutely* clear she didn't want to marry because she believed a wedding was akin to making a "claim of ownership." Ernest had grown tired of being a perpetual boyfriend and realized she wanted a relationship without rules. As if she were ashamed of him or afraid to take risks.

He didn't want to think about these mistakes, so he put them to the back of his mind. To avoid his loneliness, he played video games, studied engineering, and continued looking for a job. He didn't want to make his friends tense, and their support was important. Flipping out on them wasn't a good idea. His friends at church already had enough stress from government insisting their sermons weren't "politically correct."

It was still hard on Ernest, as he thought of her occasionally. The memories, painful though they were, also had a unique beauty to them. Unique because every person is so. The pain came from needing to work to find love again, as if he had wasted all the previous effort. They say time heals all wounds. For some, this is partly true, but some wounds are so deep, that not even scar tissue heals. Ernest felt cold, apathetic, cynical, and directionless. He needed a reason to feel happy again or at least to do more than live a blah, empty life. Not even that morning's newspaper headlines could shake his emotional deadness.

"Man Caught Masturbating in Department Store Women's Restroom. Faces Criminal Lewdness Charges." "California Governor Apologizes to Mentally Ill, Pledges State-approved Medications."

It was during this dark time, Ernest encountered... *Him.*

"You must mean *Oruaural!*"

Ernest paused in his writing to groan, "Yes, I mean you."

It was late evening, full dark. Earlier, Ernest tried dealing with his depressive mood by writing poetry and sad songs. On his way to get coffee for tomorrow, he walked down the street beside O' Tinners' Ballfield, a block away from his apartment. Which ironically Jeannette visited with Joshua for little league before they even met. Ernest told her he was never interested in sports, so he never had a reason to watch the games, but the strange connection of being so close wasn't lost on them. As if it was an omen they belonged together. Being surrounded by reminders he couldn't do anything about, was difficult. He referred to the daydreams they used to share, putting it into a song titled "One or the Other." While he didn't expect it would ever be popular, creating it seemed to help his disposition.

Verse 1
True Love is never incomplete.
No conflict in me, I asked you to marry.
Don't you see? You want to pretend, to wear your heart on your sleeve.

Chorus
Don't you know me by now? I'd stand strong, I'd be your aid, I'd run to your arms, I'd be your man.
In sickness, in health, in poverty, in wealth.
To see our lives together, to know, to feel, to hold your hand.

Verse 2
You dreamed of our smiling son in the backseat.
We wanted to see, and yet do tarry.
Did you want to trust, or yourself and I, to deceive?

Verse 3
This is to find happiness, to know without defeat.
Will my kiss on your lips, carry?
Weakness is to doubt, strength is to believe.

Verse 4
Sorrow from the fear, to send me away on my feet.
The unfulfilled desire remains imaginary?
In this do I keen, in this does my heart bleed.

Perhaps it was because of the dark feelings of frustration Ernest dwelt on, that he almost bumped into the other man. But that does not take into account the particular talents of this stranger. Like Ernest, the other man was red-haired. He wore a fine, gold-colored suit with a black tie. Oddly, he seemed extremely familiar.

"So," the stranger said, "a fine evening for coffee, eh? Oruaural prefers svarsl, but they are quite similar and might as well be the same thing."

"Do I *know* you?"

"Not as much as you actually do, but introductions are always good."

Ernest felt confused, having no idea who this person was or why they were talking to him. The other man struck a rakish pose, jauntily leaning on one leg against the ballfield's picket fence. He had an incredibly ridiculous grin on his face. Just as Ernest was about to leave, the stranger introduced himself.

"Oruaural stands before you, good sir. Or perhaps Oru-Aural, depending. *You*, however, require no introduction. Ernest and Oruaural have always known each other—about as well as the Lincoln Monument and the head on a penny. Surely, the penny knows of the Monument if it wears Lincoln's image, but if the Monument was made before that penny, how then could he know where his likeness goes? Now—"

"Uh... excuse me," Ernest interrupted, "but what do you—"

"Interruption!" With a manic pointing of his hand, and a twinkle in his eye, Oruaural interrupted right back. "Oruaural knows you wanted to ask what Oruaural meant, but you're interrupting Oruaural, so Oruaural can interrupt *you* to acknowledge that you interrupted Oruaural! Isn't Oruaural confusing? Although Oruaural is admittedly amused with the confused, Oruaural should answer your questions. Ask away!"

Having a distinct impression that the man was crazy and knowing sometimes those people can be particularly dangerous, Ernest humored him. "What exactly do you mean about the head of Lincoln and the Lincoln Monument?"

Oruaural laughed loudly. "Of *all* things to ask Oruaural, you ask about *that*? Why, it's obvious! During your life, you grew up seeing the head of Lincoln pictured on American pennies. The Lincoln Monument also honors that man, for his end to slavery, though sadly he was murdered before he could do more. Still, they both reflect that great president's honor in two different ways. At the time of our encounter, the Lincoln Monument is pictured on the back of *many* pennies, but the Monument existed long *before* them. Therefore, the Lincoln Monument did not know what would appear on the back of the penny, but presumably, the penny *does* know of the Lincoln Monument, having it on its back. Oruaural's not even trying to explain how every penny might have the Monument literally on its back, because there are so *many* pennies, and the Monument is such a big, heavy structure for all those people to carry on loose change. No, Oruaural's point is they are both related, yet different, but one does not know of the other. Like Oruaural and Ernest! Which is why Oruaural visited—yes, it is!"

Then he squared his shoulders, took a deep breath, and gave Ernest a piercing stare. "Oruaural knows that while this encounter may feel a bit strange to you, it is very important. Oruaural has need of you, and only you can help."

Ernest wanted to run away, but his curiosity compelled him to find out more. A hint of danger seemed to lurk beneath the stranger's fine suit, and undefined oddness.

He replied pointedly, "If it's illegal or dangerous, then I'm sorry, but no. What is it?"

Oruaural grinned. "Of course you would say that. Your morals are pure. That is expected. What Oruaural needs is neither illegal nor dangerous for you or anyone else. You may decline, as is your right, but why would you? Oruaural understands you may have trouble trusting a stranger, but giving you a spiel about Oruaural's trustiness distracts from the story, and Oruaural is quite prone to distraction. If you accept, Oruaural shall reward you. Your longtime girlfriend has dumped you. With no job prospects, beset with lonesomeness, your life seems porpoiseless to you. Oruaural has a porpoise and more if you will accept it. Did Oruaural mean dolphins? No! Just a play on words, although the words are *horrible* actors and actresses. Nothing at all like those irritating loopholes Arxlkarm tries with mortals."

Ernest wondered briefly if this Oruaural fellow had been stalking him, since he knew about the coffee. But how? Why? Who or *what* was Arxlkarm? Though Ernest was sure he'd never met the strange man before, the encounter felt *extremely* familiar. Unsure of how to politely dismiss Oruaural without accusing him of stalking, Ernest insisted on talking in a public place first.

"Very well!" Oruaural agreed enthusiastically. "You must've forgotten we already started talking in the *public* place that is your city's sidewalk. But you're referring to a more comfortable place to sit, and talk. Is Oruaural correct? Of course Oruaural is correct, because Oruaural is *always* correct! Except when Oruaural isn't. So to the *Public* Library of Veil we go!"

"But we're nowhere near—" Ernest was interrupted as the stranger clasped his shoulder, then just as suddenly, disappeared. They reappeared in a thoroughly darkened section of the library's parking lot, several *miles* away from where they'd been.

Ernest gasped. "How did we...?"

Oruaural chuckled with amusement. "As a gesture of Oruaural's goodwill, Oruaural chose a public place familiar to you. Whatever your decision, there's no need to be lost. Due to the peculiar nature of Oruaural, Oruaural already knows your choice. If you feel uncomfortable at the fated nature of your decision, please remember it's not *Oruaural* who's deciding. In teleporting, Oruaural showed you this is *not* the kind of random encounter you'd expect from those tabletop RPG campaigns you've seen before. It also allows Oruaural the opportunity to highlight something *important*."

"When talking with *any* Emissary—except for Arxlkarm, of course, as he'd say *anything* to get his way— you must always be specific about *exactly* what you want. Especially the rebellious ones. If you aren't, they *will* take advantage of any vagueness and use it against you. Even the 'good' ones may claim you weren't specific enough about what you wanted, therefore absolving them of any transgressions in 'misinterpreting' your request. For instance, based on what you said before, Oruaural had every right to drop you off in the very *public* location of the river, but Oruaural did not."

Flabbergasted, Ernest said, "Uh... thank you?"

"Exactly! Others may be even less concerned about what or how you feel about such things. Now come, this will be discussed with some of your peoples' coffee and delicious pie! Oruaural is paying and *absolutely* promises to behave. Oruaural doesn't want to panic anyone."

Ernest still worried about the odd man, especially over what he *just* said. Even if the stranger didn't intend to *cause* panic, hinting it was an option didn't exactly help. But he would rather talk about things inside, than in the parking lot. After selecting a table in the library's lounge, Oruaural paid for two coffees and some pumpkin pie.

Gazing with a beaming smile at his caramel cappuc- cino, as if Oruaural was about to address the coffee *instead* of Ernest, he began. "First, to explain properly, Oruaural must say what Oruaural will say, so do *not* interrupt.

Oruaural knows you have questions, and Oruaural will truthfully answer, but not if you interject. Understand?"

Ernest didn't, at least not entirely. "I... uh, I think I do?"

"Splendid!" The gold-suited man obviously wanted to clap *very* loudly but refrained. "Depending on how you perceive it, Oruaural's offer is profoundly simple yet profoundly complicated. Oruaural has need of you as an archivist, a scribe, and—" He glanced around with a knowing grin. "And for your service as a librarian. After all, how can there be a story if there is no one to tell it or keep it safe? No, don't answer that; it is but rhetorical."

"Your position will be paid, of course, in a variety of ways. For the moment Oruaural shan't explain the details. You people are sometimes concerned—or is it confused—about that thing... uh... called a spoiler alert. Though why you would be concerned about the wing on the back of one of your automobiles is beyond even Oruaural. Suffice it to say, you will find *gold* in your hands, though giving you gold also means crazy—"

Crazy? Ernest worried but kept the thought to himself.

"Oruaural means you will be *paid*, as you should be rewarded for taking dictation. You are warned though, your Earth's authorities may find this sudden possession of gold with no explainable reason to be—ahh, let's just say—suspicious. You should probably keep your treasure hidden. Speaking of which..."

Oruaural turned towards the empty air as if addressing an invisible audience. "Dear audience, there are *two* treasures hidden in this story. One is literal, physically *real* gold that even *you* might find—in a way, it is a treasure of the moment. The first can be abused in theft and perhaps encourage you to envy. But its value is defined by the reality of its existence and how much people would want all that gold. The second one is the more wonderful. Its value is defined by ambition, the desire to love, to live peacefully, and to use the first treasure fairly, but is never achieved through envy. Because of this, the value of the second far exceeds the first, so much that only one is above it in worth. Do you need a hint where our writer has hidden his gold bullion? Why, that's a basic understanding of numbers! Even if math nerds are considered squares, there is gold in them. Base it on that. Now, Oruaural must turn back to the librarian-to-be."

Addressing Ernest as if he never interrupted himself, "Before Oruaural proves the gold is yours—"

"Hey, now," Ernest interrupted. "What was that, about numbers and hidden treasure? I don't understand who you were talking to, it doesn't help me trust you."

"Oruaural wasn't talking to you, Oruaural was talking to our unseen guests! They need to know that the encrypted message is after this text. And that it's not in the 'conventional' language. And that the 'key' is before this text. And that Oruaural is rather amused by this. But now Oruaural is talking to *you* about compensation, for your acceptance. This offer will give you new purpose in your life, but it's only fair that you receive gold, as well. You need an incentive to start, like a signing bonus. Oruaural swears there will be no conditions set against you for the use of that payment, in Oruaural's realm or the rest of creation. However, as Oruaural was saying, the authorities here on your Earth may be confused about how you got so much gold so suddenly."

Ernest still felt dubious about the gold, of course. Even more so, when this odd stranger referred to Earth as if he was *visiting* it. "Earth? Are you from another planet or something?"

"More like another *something*, yes." Oruaural said this as if it were perfectly natural. "Oruaural shouldn't explain where or from *what* Oruaural comes from. You should see for yourself! After you decide to accept the job, you'll learn how to come and go from the Shifting Stones whenever you like. Oruaural doesn't want this job to interrupt your life here. You have friends and family who care about you."

Ernest noticed what sounded like a name. "So, this place you're from—you call it the Shifting Stones?"

"Ah," Oruaural answered mirthfully, "you *are* a smart one! But then Oruaural should know! The Shifting Stones is a... special sort of place, but Oruaural wants you to know how safe you'll be. Oruaural has a large number of well-armed guards. They serve Oruaural in the very same way as your peoples' police officers serve the public's justice, and one of these will answer to you personally. Additionally, your office would be in a strongly fortified location, very unlikely to be damaged during attacks... "

This talk of attacks, the need for a personal bodyguard, and "assurance" of safety actually lessened Ernest's confidence. But clearly, Oruaural had approached him nicely, as opposed to abduction via teleportation. He continued as Ernest thought about this.

"...though Oruaural personally defends the plain, as well. Those parties are particularly entertaining, so wild that they battle each other about who's the wackiest guest! For the token of that, you'd want this." Oruaural pulled out a gold ring with a large red stone set in it, "Here, this is merely a piece of unassuming fine jewelry, but in the Shifting Stones and the *other* places..."

Ernest wondered, *What does he mean,* other *places?*

"...it is the Eye of the Beholder. It grants invisibility from others at the wearer's whim and allows solid objects or spells to pass through the body. Magic, spells, and other types of energy are a topic for later discussion. You may cast both effects on yourself simultaneously. It can teleport you to certain locations in the Shifting Stones, and also *any* location within your visual sight. It does this by perceiving your thoughts. If this silly detail bothers you, I assure you it is *not* spying on you for any reason, and keeps no record of your actions. In a way, it is both a blessing and a curse. Oruaural could explain more but won't."

Irritated at not being told something, Ernest persisted. "Why not?"

Oruaural's voice took on an almost pompous quality. "Because in Oruaural's experience, lessons are best learned through... well, experience."

Parsing out the meaning, both the implied *and* stated, suggested Ernest would need to figure it out himself. "I don't want to sound ungrateful, but I'm apprehensive about the unknowns here. I—"

Oruaural frowned. "Ah, Oruaural knows what you're saying. You feel you may be jumping into danger, so you feel you're risking life and limb. Though it might be said that your limb survives by your life, but your life might not need your limb. Of course, there are risks, but there are also risks here. You might get hit by a drunken motorist, or attacked by a thief, or even hit by a world-destroying comet. To achieve anything, you must accept that risk exists and take a chance, anyway. Oruaural has seen *many* whose fear of losing their lives turns them into shut-ins with no proper life at all. You must be freely allowed to consider your fear, then choose on your own how to react to it. This is a large part of how Oruaural, as an Emissary, receives power and maintains Oruaural's influence. Remember this—choice is power, but *whose* power over *what* depends on the choice and the chooser. Will *you* choose, or let something else choose for you? The combination of your faith and free will are your greatest weapon."

The word *emissaries* bounced around in Ernest's mind until something came back to him. "You mean... *you* are one of these Emissaries you warned me about? Are you going to demand my soul?"

"Oh, but of course!" Oruaural replied with a broad grin. "Hasn't that been obvious? Not that amusing thing about your soul, it's safe... at least from Oruaural anyway. Surely after transporting in a mere *eyeblink*, you realized Oruaural was more than meets the eye? Does Oruaural look like a bus driver? Have you seen a bright yellow taxi? Is Oruaural an autobot? That was to prove what the

Emissary of Madness is, and teleporting us here demonstrated it. Oruaural *has* the power! Despite appearances, Oruaural is *not* a god or even comparable. Though Oruaural was not bound under obligation, Oruaural freely gives over Oruaural's entire self to be a servant for Ekallr's will. Oruaural represents the Shifting Stones, but is also its Master, its Mistress."

Ernest wanted to ask about that bit, but had no time, as Oruaural kept speaking without stopping, never even seeming to pause for breath.

"Oruaural would explain what that means, but Oruaural already did, power through free will, so back to the point. Oruaural came here because Oruaural needs a scribe to tell the stories of the Shifting Stones and the rest of the Fabric. But this choice can be presented only *once*, or Oruaural must look elsewhere in the omniverse." He paused to finish his coffee in one long gulp. "So, do you want to see this onetime job offer or not?"

Ernest paused for a few moments to ask his next question. "Even if I don't accept it, I can go back to my life here?"

"Yes." Oruaural grinned, as if this was all an unexpected prank. "Assuming you want to see the Shifting Stones now, that's doable. But you'd rather use the Aperture in private. *Trust* Oruaural."

"Aperture?"

"Yes," Oruaural answered. "Since your world doesn't have its own permanent gateway to the Shifting Stones, Oruaural must use a personal one. Apertures are best used privately rather than alarming others with an interdimensional portal. Oruaural doesn't wish to disturb the visitors of this elegant place of ink and letter. Libraries are more peaceful that way."

This seemed to suggest the Aperture might be frightening. Ernest wasn't sure what to expect from an interdimensional portal but had some ideas, mostly from movies. A whirling vortex of energy, wind, or lightning—probably a big disturbance for a library.

Nodding, Ernest got up. If discreetness was preferred, the nearest spot was the men's room. Instead, Oruaural led out the main doors and toward the back of the building's dumpsters. If Oruaural hadn't teleported them, Ernest would have been very suspicious of this. He wondered if maybe he still needed to be suspicious.

Suddenly, Oruaural turned around. "Another friendly warning. Remember that time you spent as a young boy, enjoying the merry-go-round? Think of that, with the whirling sights and dizziness, but instead of flying past, it's all around you with the immediate suddenness of a surprise party! Or perhaps an abrupt, unexpected amputation. You can try 'psyching yourself up' for this, but you can't really prepare for it. The more you go through this, the more you will get used to it, like learning to roller skate, or skydiving! Likewise, plain-jumping."

"Uh... maybe this is silly to ask first, but what do you mean by 'plain-jumping?'"

"Oh you're right! That *is* silly! You should have figured out by now, that plain-jumping is a more fun way of saying interdimensional travel. No more questions now, you should see Oruaural's pocket dimension. Oops!

Did Oruaural imply the idea of a world existing within Oruaural's pockets? Don't tell Gollum about it! You've got a different ring though, so maybe that won't matter."

Then without another word, Oruaural spun on his heel and faced forward again. Ernest felt a very slight push, like a blast shockwave, but much more *softer* than what he'd expected blast shockwaves to feel like. A slight but steady breeze appeared to emanate from a small, focused point ahead of Oruaural. Then he simply walked forward.

And *disappeared.*

He vanished into the air as if there was an invisible door. Ernest's only reaction was to gape at the apparent void. He saw no obvious mystical opening through reality, no gravity distortion, or anything like a wormhole.

Suddenly, Oruaural's floating head reappeared, as though peeking back through the door. "Well, mortal?! Aren't ya' coming?"

The strange shock of Oruaural's head disappearing and reappearing sent Ernest reeling, but after a moment, he gathered himself and stepped forward. A sudden dizziness struck him, and his vision blurred. Somehow, he kept his feet, though Ernest felt *more* dazed when his vision cleared.

They stood on a balcony overlooking a city. It was so massive that it covered the entirety of the horizon, but even so, only one other feature seemed to match its size. The oddness of it. Filled with all manner of bizarre shapes, the only thing it had in common with a human city was being crowded with buildings. Almost all were painted in countless colors and patterns, some so unusual Ernest couldn't make sense of them, as if Picasso and Van Gogh together designed the largest metropolis imaginable. Some buildings *moved,* swaying or even passing *through* the city itself, seemingly inspired by a living coral reef. It almost made Ernest's eyes spin again.

Some were familiar—box shapes or skyscraper-like forms—others were spheres or, more commonly, hoop-shaped. Several were unique or stood by themselves, while many sprouted in groups, or branched out like coral. Some structures completely defied description. The roads looked as confusing as the structures, so uniformly chaotic they resembled a network of termite tunnels or a subway map spread over the horizon. And that was just the cityscape. The sky was a different experience altogether.

A backdrop of inky black, it resembled the lighting of the Apollo Moon missions. Ernest couldn't see a sun, so the midday light defied logic, and despite that light, nothing cast a shadow. Dominating the sky were floating asteroids drifting like clouds. Aside from their shapes, none looked like those found in outer space. A unique environment covered each surface—deserts, forests, lakes, and even a massive, spherical sea.

Ernest couldn't even guess how far up they were, but amid the varying structure heights, there was a subtle atmospheric haze and vaporous clouds. Appearing to "swim" among the clouds were whale-like creatures trailing faint streamers of lightning. Surrounding them were faintly glowing golden lights that looked like stars,

35

but floated between his position in perspective, and the floating rocks.

As Ernest boggled at it all, Oruaural proudly declared behind him, "This is Delirium, the Shifting Stones' capital. Since this is all so different than Earth, you must be allowed some time to understand it. Explore, see the city, talk with its people, though you still need a proper guide. Please follow Oruaural."

Even with Oruaural's verbal prompting, Ernest had to be tugged along into a massively cavernous hall. The walls were slabs of solid gold so tall the Statue of Liberty might comfortably stand beside them. They were elaborately decorated with carved textural reliefs, styled as murals showing countless scenes and symbols. Ernest found himself staring at the massive golden walls, with about as much astonishment as he had for the city. Oruaural waited a moment for Ernest, then tapped his shoulder.

"Oh, mortal? Are you coming, or did you want to admire the Narrative of the Stones until Ekallr heralds his Perfection of the Fabric?"

Jumping at the shake from the surrealism, Ernest asked "Narrative?"

"Yes," Oruaural grinned. "These Walls are a historical record of the Shifting Stones. There's more to them than simply a timeline in gold, but that would diverge from the storyline. Come along now, and you'll be introduced to your guide."

Baffling as this all was, it was clearly easy to become lost, and Ernest felt overwhelmed. Naturally, he wondered if he had lost his mind. This Oruaural had implied he had an affinity for madness, after all. The wacky stranger beckoned him to what looked like a statue made of polished bronze. Its bodily form reminded Ernest of a creature in the fantasy games he played—driders. The bronze torso was a female humanoid, fused at the waist into the head of a massive spider nearly the size of a recliner chair.

The closer he got, the more the incredible detail of the statue became clear to Ernest. Not only was the torso that of a woman, but a very muscular one. The statue seemed fully articulated, like the drider wore a suit of armor instead, but the figure did *not* move, not in the slightest.

Nearly all living creatures, even if trying to hold perfectly still, make natural, subtle movements to adjust their balance, even if they aren't aware. Ernest wasn't sure if Oruaural was displaying more of his crazy side or playing a prank, but this seemed like wasting time.

"Ernest," Oruaural gestured grandly at the statue, "meet Piv, your guiding companion and personal bodyguard."

Annoyed, Ernest asked drily, "Do you mean this *statue*? I'm not trying to mock you or anything, but there's no one else here. Is Piv invisible?

Abruptly, the "statue" spoke. "No, mortal, I am not, so please do not address me as if I am not here."

Ernest staggered, while Oruaural seemed oblivious. "A wondrous marvel of engineering, is she not? The *first* thunclik Oruaural ever created, though there were many others before her. Because of Oruaural's personal hand in her creation she is, in a sense, almost a part of Oruaural.

One of the others could have been called to help, but Oruaural wants Piv here to be your guide and escort."

Piv declared proudly, "Thank you Oruaural for this opportunity to serve. I will not fail *either* of you."

"So," Oruaural continued, "now that you have a guide and guard, exploring the realm can be an afterthought for the time of the Now. A *Then*, if you can grasp it. But the context that needs discussing is the *Before*, not the *After*."

"Er... yee-es." Ernest did his best to continue, but it was difficult. "May I have a seat?"

"Ah, but of course!" Oruaural snapped his fingers, and immediately there was a noise like something flying through the air. Flying fast.

The instant he turned around, Ernest saw bits of debris whirling in the air, moving so fast he couldn't make out what they were, what to do about them, or... if they were even a threat. Then one bit dashed in toward his feet. For a brief second, it seemed about to impale his leg! Instead, it abruptly halted and settled gently on the floor, allowing Ernest to see an ornately carved piece of wood. With no time to consider this, more pieces dashed in, one after another. In less time than it takes to say "squid pie and mushroom milkshake," there was a fully assembled, richly decorated, and cushioned chair two feet away from Ernest.

Although grateful for the prompt seat, he was uncomfortable with how it had been fetched. "Ah... thank you? It's obvious you are extremely powerful, and you explained a bit why you wanted me here, but I still don't quite understand."

"Understandable."

Ernest thought, *He's definitely a few toppings short of a pizza pie, though if he doesn't scare me too much, I think I'll like him.*

"Have you ever wondered about that?" Oruaural asked "Whoever came up with making a pie of a pizza must have been thought of as crazy... *at first*! But it pleases Oru-Aural that you already think you might like me."

Ernest gasped. "You can read my thoughts? *Casually?*"

Oruaural seemed to ignore the exclamation. "Making a pizza pie is like combining two different things that seemed to have *no* connection with each other... until you're putting them together. You've heard of combining peanut butter and chocolate to make candy? Well, have you ever heard of a chocolate-filled tube worm? Or peanut butter and vinegar cream? But you're correct, you do need to know more about Oruaural's intentions, as you mortals get concerned about the silliest things. You know Oruaural is powerful, but not *why*. Yet you came here anyway! Don't ya think that's a bit risky? Well? Don't ya'? That's because it is! And when merrily prancing through your mind, wouldn't it be fun if," his voice dropped ominously low, "you should know how Oruaural is not just insane, but has been known to act on it. Not that Oruaural is making another wacky play on words, because that's what this is, without even casting rehearsals too! But this is also to remind you that Oruaural has been known for some **crazy** antics..."

Ernest began to wonder about the depth of what he'd gotten into, but Oruaural continued. "Now, you're starting to wonder about the depth of what you got yourself into. Oruaural's job is simple: to provide care and protection for the insane, and, if possible, to contain them here until they've recovered. If they don't, well that's mitigated, too. You should know by now that Oruaural is also a patient, to paraphrase the commercial. You, your job is simple. On Earth, few people know of this universe and its stories. Why, what good is a toadstool, if the toad isn't even sitting on the stool? That's your job, Ernest."

"My job is making sure toads use mushrooms as furniture?"

"No, of course not!" Oruaural laughed long and loud. "Unless you're saying you want a hobby? No, Oruaural needs you to tell the stories of this alternate universe. If Oruaural asked one of Oruaural's wonderfully loyal-to-the-death-in-the-most-furious-of-ways followers to spread the glory of this story to your world, they absolutely would!"

His voice suddenly became shrill and angry. Though Ernest couldn't understand who or what Oruaural was angry with, as if the Emissary's frustration was against a situation rather than a person. It was obvious to Ernest that none of the body language or shouting was intended against him.

"But they do not understand Earth any more than you understand the Shifting Stones, let alone Aerth. Being the way they are, if they didn't wind up dissected in a laboratory, they might be dismissed as harmlessly crazy. Or go on a bloodthirsty killing spree. Either way, the stories wouldn't be heard, and surely Oruaural absolutely,

positively, categorically, definitely, unquestionably, will...
not... have... that!"

His voice returned to normal. "No, Oruaural didn't
call you Shirley. In this universe, Emissaries are the incarnated expression of feeling, of those themes that affect
creation the most. They gain power the more that mortals
do or say something related to the Emissaries. Therefore,
in writing this story, Oruaural gets stronger when your
people sympathize with Oruaural for defending the mentally unbalanced from themselves and their disorders.
The audience should also know that your job will be to
take the audience's questions and relay them for Oruaural
to answer. Doubtless they will have some."

Ernest frowned. "Take the audience's questions? How
will I do that, if I'm here?"

Oruaural laughed. "Because that's the author's prerogative, obviously!"

"If *I'm* going to write this," Ernest asked, "doesn't that
make it *my* prerogative?"

"Yes, if *you* are the author." Oruaural smiled know-
ingly. "There's only one thing Oruaural can say about
that—you're an 'avatar,' of sorts. The Fourth Window
will explain what that's all about when you get to it, but
Oruaural will not. Oruaural should stay with the current
part of the narrative. You have another question, don't
you? About Earth's humans sympathizing with Oruaural?"

"Yes... that's still uncomfortable. How you know those
things. Um, doesn't sympathizing mean—in the way you
describe it—that you *are* 'feeding' from Earth's emotional energy?"

"No!" Oruaural groaned. "Oruaural knew ahead of time what you would say, yet still feels angry about the misunderstanding. Each Emissaries' strength of power starts at a base level given to them at their creation by Ekallr, who created us to serve and administer his will for creation. Some rebelled, not respecting the authority of their maker, or believing their ideas were better for creation than Ekallr's."

"Ekallr?"

"Yes." Oruaural nodded. "For lack of a better metaphor, he's the creator of the universe. Perhaps even the same being you know as creator, though that's never been understood, even by the most loyal of Emissaries. When the Emissaries were created, they were given a base starting level of strength that can never decline. That power is amplified by mortals who behave according to the nature of the Emissary, even if the emotions are sourced from another universe. It's quite complicated to describe properly, so Oruaural will merely call it a bleed-through effect. No matter what you mortals do or say, each of you behaves in a way that amplifies at least one Emissary. Take color, for example. If you have a diluted dab of green paint, then add more of the same, the dab becomes more intense, yes? More opaque?"

Ernest frowned. "How is that *not* feeding on emotion?"

"Because feeding implies absorption. Instead, when emotional energy is generated in sympathizing with a character like Oruaural, it amplifies Oruaural's power as the mortals align to it. The energy is not absorbed, but it does help with a boost. Since that power is most concentrated in the Shifting Stones, Oruaural wanes when Oruaural is away from Oruaural's realm. Anyhoo, Oruaural knows you have one particularly important question, so ask away."

Ernest blinked. He wasn't thinking about any specific question, but as he thought about it, one did come to mind. "Why are you talking about *me* writing a story? It's as if you're saying I've already accepted your offer."

Piv suddenly chortled, much like a steam whistle. It made Ernest jump because she had been so quiet.

"Piv." The golden-suited man turned to her. "You know very well this is a necessary part of the process. Explaining this to Ernest is important, even if you do find it silly. Oruaural made you, recovered the Tapestry's Fragment, and defended The Shifting Stones as its rightful Ruler. Though Oruaural has no inches or metric marked on Oruaural as the ruler—but that's beside the point. Is there anything *else* you find amusing?"

"No, my Monarch." Hiding her mirth was still evidently difficult. Wisps of steam rose from Piv's back and face, which wore a stifled grin. The metallic, flute-like voice clearly had laughter in it.

"Good." Oruaural's attention returned to Ernest. "Oruaural doesn't want interruptions while Oruaural talks about this. It's as important as the way an adorable little girl pleads to hug a puppy... or was it the way the puppy fears being hugged to death? Ah, sometimes those cartoons were *so* amusing! Now, Ernest, your question is simply answered by saying three things. One—Oruaural needs a written account of Oruaural's story, or else it is unknown and invisible. Two—knowledge is power; as Oruaural said before, Oruaural gains more power when more people sympathize. And three—you've already written the story, *you just don't know it yet!*"

Ernest was discomforted by that last part but dismissed it as simply another aspect of Oruaural's madness.

"Um..." the future scribe asked, "I'm standing here now, not writing anything. How could you say I've 'already' written this?"

"Oruaural *already* answered this question, so Oruaural's not going to again. Oruaural knows this may not be satisfactory, but explicitly insists these details shouldn't be explained for now. All will be revealed later anyway, and Oruaural is teasing your interest along."

Though Ernest wanted to keep figuring out his strange new situation, the human displaced from Earth felt exhausted. Oruaural could tell, of course, since he had approached Ernest in his late evening. A full day in the Shifting Stones is thirty-two hours long, as opposed to Earth's twenty-four—an extra eight hours. Ernest yawned and asked Oruaural where he could sleep.

Oruaural jumped up. "Of course! Please follow Oruaural and mind the golden lights!"

Ernest followed Oruaural through a twisting labyrinth of hallways. As they walked forward, a series of lights appeared to guide them ahead and disappeared after their passing. Oruaural and Piv both seemed to follow them, so Ernest concluded these were the "golden lights." He was glad for the directions they indicated because every passage looked alike, and there were *many*. These invoked concerns of being hopelessly lost without the lights. Lacking windows, the halls felt enclosing but not quite claustrophobic.

Before long, they stood at a broad door, lit by a small gas fire fed by a pipe. The flame seemed unusually straight to Ernest as it streamed off the fixture. Also, it was green, and the area seemed more illuminated than possible.

Oruaural swept his arm grandly, as though he were a game show host with a face-splitting grin. "Ernest, this is your room. You may use it however you wish, whether that means installing a plasma TV set or bolting your furniture to the ceiling. As Oruaural pointed out before, your freely chosen decision is *that* important. Besides, forced decisions are usually unfair. Oruaural wants you to have time to understand why you would accept Oruaural's offer, and why you would feel comfortable with it."

Ernest missed most of that as he stared at the "room." One could easily build a small *house* in it, the room was that big. It seemed almost like a manmade cave. A... mancave. Ernest was speechless again, for a moment. Then he blurted, "This is *my* room?"

Oruaural grinned. "No, this is where Oruaural practices dancing a jig on the side of the wall. The thunclik make for lovely partners, *especially* with their arachnid footwork. Joking aside, as a mortal, you have needs, including sleep, food, and privacy."

Next as he'd done with that chair, Oruaural "threw together" a full set of apartment furniture. For a living room, kitchenette, bedroom, and bathroom, all to Ernest's preferences. Particularly confusing were the sink and bath/shower which had no plumbing fixtures or visible ways of providing water. Sending servants to fetch jugs seemed frivolous for someone who could literally bend this place to his will. But Oruaural certainly wouldn't see to the, uh... bathroom necessities. Would he?

"Ernest?" Oruaural tapped the human's shoulder. "It may be a bit, ah... different from what you're used to, but this *is* your room, as much as..." He stared vacantly as if in deep thought. "Why, it's yours as much as your brave red heart! Do with it what you like. You may even eat it. Oruaural means the room, of course. You can't eat your own heart—you'd die! So, please don't try."

Ernest finally had a reply. "I... won't. But I'm wondering, if there's no plumbing, how do I use the sink and the... uh..."

Oruaural blinked, pretending ignorance while drawing out a long "Yeee-ess?"

Annoyed, Ernest asked the obvious. "How do I use the bathroom?"

"That's easy! Just stick your hands in it!"

Ernest deadpanned, "Stick my *what* in *what*?"

"Your hands!"

He guided Ernest over to the sink and tugged his hands into it. As if from thin air, a dense cloud of mist coalesced in the basin, and the human felt water beading thickly on his fingers.

Delightedly, Oruaural explained. "Magic may not be plentiful on Earth, but that's what this is. Simply use the sink, bath, shower, and of course, the toilet, for the intended purpose. They'll take care of themselves;

motion-sensing magic is fairly easy to use. Piv will be near the door if you need anything. Later, she will introduce you to Oruaural's realm. Goodnight. Oruaural will see you in the morning."

He and Piv left. The thunclik guard seemed to have a coy grin, but Ernest felt too tired to ask why. Twenty minutes later, despite the niggling concern that he may actually be insane, Ernest had undressed and was sound asleep.

QUADRANT TWO:

TRAINING THE LENS OF REFLEX

Know thyself and thou shall know preparedness.

– The Sword of the Hand, by Rytoss, 1st Master of the Calm-Tornado fighting style

N ext Ernest slept of course, and dreamed about his life. Oruaural urged Ernest to write about it. Obviously that's difficult for the dreamer to do while they're asleep. So Ernest wrote this out while he was awake, though you must've known that already. Right?

When Ernest woke after this dream, Oruaural told him to write it into the story, despite how the human felt uncomfortable with the dream's content. Oruaural's point was that describing it could help Ernest recognize what caused his distress and might lead to dealing with his feelings. And it was about his first night and all. Sorta like celebrating the launching of a ship. Oruaural even assured him that he wouldn't need the wine bottle to be smashed over his head either. No need to waste a perfectly good bottle of wine after all. What follows is Ernest's dream recalling his life, his difficulties finding a job, and the possibility of his suicide. Thankfully, Oruaural had intervened to change *that* dark spiral.

Now that it's been established the following is a dream, Oruaural is wondering why the audience is lingering on this sentence and not reading the description of the dream below. Is it because Oruaural is chatty? Oruaural will be quiet now.

There were many subjects Ernest found interesting in school: history, science, astronomy, art, and books—from *Great Expectations* to *Flash Gordon*. At fifteen years old, his parents sent him to an institution for behavioral examination where he was diagnosed with high-functioning autism. The disorder meant he was easily distracted and had great difficulty understanding emotional subtlety. It reinforced another talent, though.

When Ernest doodled or daydreamed, his imagination became a vast universe of amusing things to entertain him. He drew bombers in aerial combat, made a biplane with bits of paper and glue on a whim, pretended to adventure on a lava-strewn alien world, or imagined meeting the Green Knight of the Arthurian epic. Unfortunately, his imagination didn't help him stand up against bullies.

In high school, this creativity helped with art class, as his doodles became more detailed. He became fascinated with blueprints, engine designs, pumps, and other complex machines. The local school system had something called the Vocational Industrial Training and Occupation Center, or VITOC. The Center provided students with a realistic workplace experience and aided them toward becoming independent adults. Initially, Ernest thought about becoming a mechanic, but pursued computer-aided drafting instead.

Unfortunately, his lack of social skills prevented him from establishing a rapport with anyone he approached for jobs. The mechanics never explained why they turned him down; the few returned calls were polite rebuffs. He interviewed for job after job but found nothing better than temporary labor. Hoping to boost his qualifications, Ernest pursued an Associate's degree in engineering at the Oregon campus of the Woodlimb Institute for Technology or "WIT". Even though he made a serious study of the subject, he found calculus beyond his comprehension.

Ernest was lonely. He longed desperately to find companionship. Every woman he approached wanted him to have a job, perhaps falling prey to society's expectations of a "reliable man." He hated the lonesomeness he felt, but unpleasant as it was, he felt more haunted by inferiority, an honest acknowledgement in how difficult higher mathematics was. Engineering firms needed competency, not an inability to read even simple functions for accelerating velocity. He still accepted this was no excuse to give up on an income, and kept looking for work. He was certain he could succeed as an office assistant, who could at least understand CAD drawings.

But the dream didn't *start* with the background of his life, because all that was memory. The dream started with a cold downpour trickling little streams of rain down the window next to him. He sat on the city's transit rail looking for yet another engineering firm's office, anxiety threatening failure again. Breakfast wasn't settling well, but at least this time he remembered his suit for the interview. Even though he had been refused many times already, he persisted with hopes for a position in an engineering office.

Stepping off the train, everything changed. The dream shifted to Ernest's apartment. It was a mess—papers, clothes, and garbage everywhere. The sink was piled with dishes and smelled strongly of mold. He still had the same dingy couch Jeannette left him, though its old striped pattern was barely visible under the stains now. He desperately wanted to get rid of it, but most new couches would require a year's savings. With this inconvenient reminder of her, there were times he wondered if some part of Jeannette's personality *wanted* him to commit suicide.

It looked like Ernest hadn't cleaned in years, as if nothing there seemed to matter to him anymore. The drafter's portfolio he needed for job interviews was buried under some dusty pants and a pile of cans. It smelled faintly of beer. Had he given up on his career?

The calendar still had therapy appointments and some days marked "job search." No drafting firm interviews. There was also a conspicuous frowny face on September twenty-third. The day at the Quesa Mesa, when Ernest met Jeannette and started dating her.

Suddenly, the calendar started flipping ahead on its own, the months flying away, as if time had fast-forwarded. Ernest's face in the bathroom mirror grew colder, harsher, more cynical. In the hallway, the old calendar was replaced with a new one, the months flying by but fewer appointments appearing on it. Even the therapy reminders and church volunteering disappeared. Year after year, the apartment's only change was an increase in messiness. Then, it abruptly stopped—September again. This time the twenty-third was marked with one word.

Death.

Ernest stared for a few seconds, then turned to the door. After he stepped through, the dream changed again.

Now he stood on the sidewalk of the I-36 highway bridge, better known as the Grey Span, crossing the river between Veil and Boston. Ernest gave no indication why he was there, though the scene was suffused with an eerie sense of horripilation. He stepped toward the highway department's access ladder and began to climb the rungs. Despite his dream of becoming an engineer, this did *not* look like a bridge inspection for faults or cracks. This looked like a man climbing a bridge's superstructure with no concern for the girders beyond how high up they went.

As Ernest looked around on the upper trusses, the bridge's lift operators set the road barricades, blocking traffic. Obviously trying to prevent something terrible, one of the operators approached Ernest on the catwalk. Ernest ignored him and jumped.

The nightmare ended with the bridge operator screaming as Ernest struck the road deck.

As she approached the human's new quarters, Piv heard terrified screaming through the door. The thunclik suddenly reshaped her right arm into a sharp and deadly longsword. The other became a huge shield, edged with the teeth of a saw. It covered half of her torso and her arachnid forelegs. The sawtooth edges buzzed as Piv slammed the shield into the door, tearing it apart.

After finding Ernest was the one screaming in his sleep. Piv rushed to the bed, reshaping her sword back into an arm. Then she shook him awake. "Wake up!"

Ernest looked up blearily, then fear jolted him awake. As he scrambled away from her and out of bed, he gestured to Piv's sawtooth-edged shield. "Why did you hold that above my head and loom over me? You looked like you were about to bash me in my sleep!"

"I had no intention of assaulting you," the ferocious-looking metal woman replied. "I heard screaming, so I thought you were being attacked. Speaking of which, I don't see a threat. Did you want me to pulverize your door, or were you pulling my leg?"

"No," Ernest answered incredulously. "If you could tell I was having a nightmare, why are you asking about my door?"

"Because I was trying to cheer you up. I'm sure your body is still flooded with adrenaline and residual stress. Do you want some time to relax?"

Ernest looked at her and thought. His nightmare bothered him, as any would, though it seemed unusual. The calendar, the way things changed in the dream. He wasn't sure what it meant exactly, but the advancing of time might've represented his future. Ernest still wondered why though, because he didn't feel so depressed he'd commit suicide. Not to mention, he didn't expect that to happen if he remained in this... alien world? Alternate dimension?

"Piv, I want to speak with Oruaural about my nightmare. I—"

"Yes, my Lord." Piv's eyes flashed with white light. "We're—"

It confused him that Piv referred to him as Lord. Shouldn't that title apply to Oruaural? "Piv, why did—"

"Shush, my Lord is talking to me."

Ernest frowned. "What? I'm not—"

Piv held up a finger to her lips, then nodded and smiled. "Yes, my Lord. No, I haven't had time to ask him, but I think he's ready for the demonstration."

Piv paused, obviously listening for some instructions Ernest wasn't hearing. She nodded again and smiled broadly. "Yes, my Lord. That will be my *pleasure*. I am honored by your order. I will help him to prepare."

"What?" Ernest asked, a little uncomfortable with Piv's broad grin. "What's going on?"

"I was instructed to tell you Oruaural also wishes to speak with you about your nightmare. Because of Oruaural's awareness of our relative positions in this moment, my Emissary will summon and manifest us directly to the throne room."

"What does that mean?"

"That means I put my hand on your shoulder," which Piv did, "then Oruaural locates my signal. Earth's sci-fi has depicted teleportation, yes?"

"Yes, but—"

"Good. You already know what's going on then! Oruaural, beam us up!"

Ernest still felt confused, but before he could ask for further clarification, he experienced a sudden queasiness. Then his bedroom transitioned abruptly into the bizarre cityscape Oruaural had presented to him yesterday. The scene perspective looked much the same as before, so he expected it was the same balcony. Turning his head, he saw the same towering golden walls covered in pictographs. But if this was Oruaural's throne room, it now looked much different. The first time, it appeared to be constructed of a nondescript polished stone. Now everything looked "made" of liquid gold, if apparently solid forms could ripple and flow in apparently solid shapes. The throne had been replaced by... a freestanding coatrack?

Ernest furrowed his brow. "Is there a special reason why your throne room—"

"This isn't a throne room!" Oruaural laughed. "It's a reflection of Oruaural's current state of mind. Though the different political parties of Oruaural's mind often vote against each other, personal appearance and throne room décor are two things they can agree on multilaterally. Just remember, Oruaural is absolutely bonkers. Now, if you'd like to see a throne room..."

In an instant, the entire room reshaped itself into a modern bathroom. Staring bewilderedly, Ernest experienced a sort of sensory upheaval combined with a feeling both surreal and ineffable. Oruaural, now seated on his golden bathroom "throne," continued.

"To address the obvious implication, yes, Oruaural could have visited you in your room but wanted you to see the demonstration of the throne room, and of teleportation. However, that does not explain *how* it was all done. Besides, this discussion on magic is as much for our audience as it is for you. Ernest, are you familiar with the double-slit experiment?"

"Yes?"

"Well," Oruaural said, "that double-slit experiment is a minor example of how practical reality and "sorcery" blend together. Craziness in physics! Personally, Oruaural feels flattered. Or dismayed? In the first version of the experiment, scientists pointed a single laser at two openings in a precision-cut metal strip. Please tell Oruaural, how many shadows would you expect to appear from light shining through *two* holes?"

Ernest wondered if this was a trick question, but still answered. "Two?"

Oruaural shook his head. "You'd expect that, but no. Try eight, or even twelve."

"What?"

"More than two appeared, definitely more than made sense. The light seemed to 'interfere' with itself. It would've scared the daylights out of Earth's Isaac Newton. It certainly spooked Einstein. Do you know what creates laser light? Electron particles. The next idea the scientists tried, was to observe *which* electrons went through *which* hole. This is where reality as you know it and the unknown mix together. Take another guess how many shadows appeared when they played peekaboo."

Ernest thought about it again, but if the experiment defied the first expectation of *two* stripes of light, he wasn't sure. "I don't know. Um... thirteen? It's unlucky, right?"

Oruaural laughed. "No. When the movements of the electrons were carefully observed, only then did the outlines of the two holes appear. The scientists weren't able to understand how or why the laser light interfered with itself, but they found that observation played a role in this, as if consciousness itself affected the patterns. Your scientists still don't know how or why, because that's a *secret*. It helps point out what can be done with consciousness. If you're able to focus your awareness with your intentions to a solid belief of the possibilities of subatomic matter, it allows you to choose those possibilities. That is what you might call magic, Ernest. But to *affect* it requires a mastery of discipline and intention from mortals, because choosing the conditions of subatomic matter affects what is *made* of subatomic matter. Science as you know it, can't explain this, so that's enough of an explanation for now. As Oruaural said, your Earth's Einstein found this 'spooky.' Ironically, after formulating his famous theory of relativity, Einstein spent the rest of his life trying to find a scientific expression for everything. Ironic, because quantum entanglement is a fundamental part of what he sought, especially for more than just a particle coupling. The unified field theory is the substance of 'magic', but to manipulate it by disciplined thought requires an innate personal awareness of the subatomic behavior of your subject. Unfortunately, conscious awareness of everything else distracts this focus, plus you have to believe in things that seem... *crazy.*"

Ernest wasn't sure what to make of this. Was magic possible for a simple mortal like himself? If so, how did one train for that? The only real examples he heard regarding what science couldn't explain, were impressive only because science couldn't explain them. Whether extinguishing candles by concentrating on them or telekinetically moving a spoon without touching it, both apparently cost a great deal of personal energy for the effort.

"Are you saying," Ernest wondered aloud, "that if I disciplined my mind... I'd... be able to... to cast fireballs or lightning from my hands? Like from... a fantasy story?"

Oruaural clapped loudly. "You're already in a fantasy story. Look around, you're literally conversing with a mad incarnation of madness! Though, admittedly, this is all for Oruaural to serve the greater will of Oruaural's creator, Ekallr. As for magic, fire or lightning are excellent examples! Hot or cold is really just a matter of atoms vibrating more or less, respectively. What becomes hot must also have cold! Lightning is simply a surge of electrons passing from their ground state to a target with a compelling positive charge. But that's not the magic lesson Oruaural wanted you to learn, because Einstein would have found it just as spooky as quantum entanglement. Why are you even bringing up Einstein? Oruaural's not interested in him right now!"

Flustered, Ernest said, "I didn't bring up Einstein. You—"

"Yes, quite right, Ernest!" Oruaural laughed even louder than he clapped. "Thank you for finishing

Oruaural's thought! Oruaural wants to help you understand your nightmare. Before that, Oruaural needs to look at your motivations."

"Have I done something wrong?" Ernest wondered if Oruaural doubted his intentions. He felt no loyalty toward the odd man, yet felt no ill intentions.

"No." Oruaural smiled warmly. "You've done nothing wrong. You should know this realm is an extension of Oruaural, so nothing that displeases Oruaural can act against Oruaural within its borders. Even if Oruaural allowed such things to attack, they cannot overpower what Ekallr grants Oruaural in the Shifting Stones! Haha! Only Ekallr has the ability to override Oruaural here! That is his prerogative, as creator of the Fabric. No, Oruaural doesn't doubt you, Ernest. Though you do not know why, Oruaural considers you one of Oruaural's most important friends. Oruaural wants to look at your motivations so that *you* know your own motivations. If you know your motives are truly righteous, then by this, you seek after the kingdom of righteousness and are fortified by that strength. Do you know what your future would have been like if Oruaural had *not* encountered you?"

Ernest recalled his nightmare. "Uh... yes. I... uh..." He remembered how Oruaural seemed to read his mind yesterday. On cue, he answered the unspoken question.

"No, Oruaural doesn't know all of the details of your timeline. That's *your* timeline, *not* Oruaural's. But Oruaural *does* know of your nightmare, and that was a plausible future. You realize now you don't *really* want to kill yourself. Though you probably would have tried later, because your despair was for unfulfilled companionship. You realized Jeannette would continue rejecting you, and trying again was emotionally unhealthy for you *and* her. You want to move on but haven't realized yet how to separate the specific feeling of love from your memory of Jeannette. If you had not met Oruaural, you would have needed a fulfilling purpose for your life to avoid suicide. Without Oruaural, you needed several things—love with another woman, a job to which you could apply your education, and to grow more sociable. Becoming more practical, more optimistic—smell the flowers, nurture a passion for something you love, and perhaps spiritual comfort with church. Unfortunately, sometimes this is difficult, finding that happy balance. But Oruaural *did* visit you. The pertinent motivations here and now are simple. What you risk your life for, if called to it?"

Before Ernest could reply, Oruaural pointed his hand in front of him. A tortured hellscape of metal pipes, machinery, smoke, fiery lava, and bones appeared. The vision had fuzzy edges, so Ernest expected whatever Oruaural conjured up, it was a window to some awful place.

"That," Oruaural said, "is the Mire of Worms. Depending on who you ask, it is the personal realm or prison of Bu' Zast, Emissary of Devastation. He does *everything* in the evilest way possible. No varying shades of grey, only whips, chains, cages, and worse. Without kinkiness in mind! Bu' Zast believes strength and power are the only things worthy of existence. Because these attributes are pursued easily by evil, he derives his existence by personally—or through his followers—inflicting needless pain, torture, and death, or even worse, *blue neckties!*"

"Neckties?" Ernest had no idea how this related to anything.

Oruaural frowned harshly, his voice a deep, angry growl. "You do **not** want to know."

Wisely, Ernest moved on. "Okay, you're right—I don't. I understand you probably have personal reasons to hate this... Bu' Zast, but you were talking about *my* personal reasons. If I've never heard of him, then I have no reason to... uh, hate him. I mean, Emissary of Devastation sounds bad, but I don't have any context. He doesn't demand blood sacrifices from his cultists, does he?"

Oruaural slapped his stomach. "You have such silly notions, Ernest! Blood sacrifices, haha! Why, that's a great idea for a banquet!"

Piv interjected, "Bu' Zast sees things like poverty and weakness as imperfections in Ekallr's creation. He is so devoted to 'fixing' the omniverse, he'd destroy those 'imperfections' by purging them from creation. He constantly tries to make war with everyone and everything."

"Indeed!" Oruaural chuckled. "To force or impose his will over the 'mistakes' of creation. Which to Bu' Zast, means destroying anyone or anything who disagrees with him, even if they don't know about him. Maybe even destroying some who *do* agree with him. Each Emissary pursues behavior aligned to their nature. Naturally, this encourages their followers to, well... follow in similar behavior. Which sounds counterintuitive, as Oruaural is the Emissary of Madness and works to provide recovery.

More or less. Oruaural might do something on the relatively low end of insanity, such as calmly describing to you an alternate dimension. Or Oruaural might send a troop of pink elephants dancing through here at any second!"

Oruaural shouted this last with such sudden loudness and emotional overtone that Ernest backed up. He almost expected a hallucination of that very scene from the animated film *Dumbo*.

"Bu' Zast on the other hand," Oruaural continued, "is the Emissary of Devastation. Not only does his title sound bad, he also does *everything* at the most extreme level of badness! No calm chats about how to eviscerate an army marching against him, no dancing through sprinkled intestines—no, he does *everything* in the most extreme way he can! There is no ten percent with Bu' Zast, not even what's expected at one hundred percent; there's only infinity percent and he *never* accepts failure. Ever! It's why even some of the more evil-ish Emissaries hate him. So, now that you know why you'd want to fight him—"

"Um... excuse me, Oruaural?" Ernest said cautiously. "This all may be why *you* would fight him, but not why *I* would."

"Of course it's why you would fight him." Oruaural gave Ernest a piercing stare. "Didn't Oruaural mention Bu' Zast has been secretly trying to manipulate Earth's mortals into aligning with his influence? And that he's already preparing an army to sweep over, not only Aerth, but also the Earth you know?"

"Um... no." Ernest was taken aback, unsure if he could believe it. "I'm certain you didn't mention that. Given all the... ahh, strange things I've seen you do, I'm unsure how to take this. I'll grant I've seen you're capable of *many* things, none of them easy to overlook or forget. I'm sure if this Bu' Zast or his followers were meddling on Earth, someone would have noticed by now."

"You think so, do ya?" Oruaural's grin widened. "What if Oruaural told you this... isn't... even... Oruaural's... *final form!*"

"What?" Ernest's eyebrow was raised over his other eye's squint.

"Piv?" Oruaural gestured. "Please show him your human side."

Ernest turned and didn't see Piv. Instead, he saw an average-looking blonde human woman in blue jeans and a gray T-shirt. The sudden surreality of seeing another human being increased, when the strange woman's body morphed from a Caucasian into a Latina, then an African, then an Asian. Her body's size and build didn't change, but her facial characteristics and skin color did. It was so fast and unusual that Ernest struggled to comprehend.

"How?" It was all he could manage.

The strange, uncanny woman still had Piv's voice. "What?" She asked impishly. "Can't a girl have some fun with her outfits? Haven't you noticed how Oruaural can do all manner of things that defy your expectations of science and even of magic?"

Oruaural added. "Some of our audience must have already figured this out, but Oruaural is *not* human, nor bound by typical mortal constraints. This means Oruaural's operatives have the ability to avoid being discovered by the forces of evil. Oruaural's reason for appearing to you as a human on Earth was to avoid a 'freak out.' If Oruaural terrified you that first time, what do you think you would have done? Unnecessary violence would have destroyed all that we're doing now, and your nightmare would probably have happened instead."

"So," Ernest pondered aloud, "what exactly is your final form?"

"Good question!" The Master of Madness laughed. "Oruaural understands why you would ask, and Oruaural doesn't mind. However, if Oruaural revealed Oruaural's preferred appearance, it would ruin part of our narrative. That's part of why our audience is enjoying this story of *how* Oruaural became Oruaural."

Having resumed her metallic arachnid form, Piv spoke, drawing Ernest's attention. "Earth has many fantastic stories to explain what people do not easily understand. Some may have been from people who were mad or saw things they didn't understand for other reasons. But some stories of leprechauns, werewolves, vampires, witches, knights slaying dragons, houses with chicken legs, or various other cultural pantheons, were inspired by what you see here. Or the 'others.'"

Ernest frowned in concentration. "So, Earth's folklore is based on visits from interdimensional aliens? And, what 'others' do you mean?"

"To answer your first question, yes!" Oruaural cried happily, then cried sadly, "And No! But to answer your second question, Oruaural is not the *only* Emissary, as you'll find out more on your adventure."

Piv clarified, "Indeed, some of Earth's folklore have no connection to the Emissaries or their servants, but it has had visits from them—some benign, others malignant. Your history is not overwhelmed by the more malicious Emissaries, mainly because they are rebuffed by the powerful combination of free will and religious belief. Faith-based morals, with humanity's innate adherence to conscience, help prevent humans from aligning with evil. It doesn't prevent it completely, because to have true free will, the option must be present. Although this means Earth is substantially resistant to evil influence, free will trends toward evil, because the desire for oneself encourages theft or murder. Whatever the self wants, it will try to obtain if morals aren't considered, even if this may grievously harm others to obtain those wants. When this is common, it aligns with the rebellious Emissaries. For example, they spread panic and persecution during the Dark Ages, in the French Revolution, and in similar situations. Recently, they have been using a new tactic."

Oruaural howled with rage. "The rebellious ones' latest scheme tricks people into believing that lies are truth! That *nothing* is immutable! That tyranny 'knows better' than the people! If they throw a bunch of honey into the pot, the flies will stick to it, which lures the frogs to gobble them up. Then when the water starts heating slowly, the frogs don't want to leave their flies behind, do they? No, they're quite comfortable letting themselves get cooked. Then it's frog dinner for everyone *but* the frogs!"

"Okay," Ernest said. "What are these evil things they're doing to trick us?"

Oruaural shook his head. "Oh, no... no, no, no. It's too early to tell them what the flies are. Oru-Aural wants them to figure that out for themselves, as they read about the adventure! Besides, you still need to know how to use the ring. Oruaural will help you expose the flies of the evil ones, but not if you refuse, naturally."

Ernest sighed. He had to acknowledge that whatever Oruaural was, he was more than capable of defying any law of physics. He might be lying, to manipulate Ernest into agreeing, but he did have a point. If Oruaural's implication of *other* Emissaries visiting Earth was correct, then they might very well have powerful abilities and cryptic motives of their own. He decided he needed to see for himself what these Emissaries might have in mind for Earth, especially if they'd been influencing behavioral trends. Then he would decide what to do about it.

"So," Ernest said, "you knew that I'd accept anyway?"

"Absolutely!" Oruaural beamed. "But as Oruaural said earlier, before hurling you out into the unknown, you need to use your protection!"

"Protection? What's a condom got to do with—"

Mortified, Oruaural furiously shook his blushing head. "No, not *that* kind of protection. You need to know how to use the Eye of the Beholder, the ring Oruaural gave you. Oruaural doesn't want to describe the mischief—" An abrupt growl. "—of the *rhinos.*" Then exuberantly, "That's for later!"

Ernest was immediately sure he didn't want to know anything about "mischief" involving rhinoceroses, so he quickly asked, "Is the ring difficult to use? Is there something important I need to do?"

"You'll see! Just remember, it's tied in with your perception! Now, Piv! Buy yourselves some breakfast at the market. Go have fun with him!" He gleefully shouted this with a long peel of maniacal laughter.

Ernest felt uneasy about much that Oruaural had already said and done. Now the wild, reality-bending Master of Madness was referring to the ring. While laughing maniacally.

As they walked through Oruaural's palace, Piv explained about the disguises. Each was a set of selections of holographic skin and clothes applied over her metal body. Underneath, her body's huge spidery form was close to an easy chair in size. That suggested her arachnid chassis should have been poking out underneath her "hips". But earlier, no bronze metal was visible, and the appearance was convincing. If Ernest hadn't known better, he'd never have believed she was actually a woman made of bronze metal underneath. If her hologram was "bigger on the inside," was that non-Euclidian geometry?

Ernest wondered about the Eye of the Beholder, now on his finger. He knew they said the ring was special and was impatient to ask about it.

"Are you going to tell me anything about this ring?"

"Not right now," Piv stonewalled.

"Wait until we get there, then?"

"Yes."

Ernest sighed with resigned frustration, accepting that he'd understand more later. Giving in to his body's need for sleep last night, there hadn't been an opportunity to explore the Shifting Stones, or even meet anyone else. Now he could look forward to this, at least.

Along the way, the stranger in a strange land noticed strange people mingling in the strange identical hallways. Ernest saw bat-like Vungir with vulpine heads resembling the flying fox, Earth's largest bat species. The creatures had long, flattened tails that appeared to aid in flying. Though the ball-shaped Quastrans were about as tall as Ernest, they had a chitinous exoskeleton like that of a three-legged, three-armed crab. The four-legged insectoid Thvenel looked like giant mantidflies, a cross between a yellow hornet and a mantis, but without the scythes. The Tasdo reptilians were covered head to tip-of-serpentine tail in toughened scales, half-snake, half-humanoid. The Aejlii were even weirder, looking like a combination of cat, fish, and... frog?

When he realized he was the only human there, Ernest felt unnerved. All these people seemed curious about him, staring as if they had never seen a human before, but apparently most weren't interested in small talk or asking about the human. After navigating the hallways for a half hour, they arrived at the market.

In the plaza, Piv talked with a Tasdo food vendor at his stall. While getting a closer look, Ernest noted more resemblance to the fantasy creature of a *naga*, with a snake-tail and humanoid torso covered in reptilian features. The serpentine man had sharp-looking viper fangs and saw-like teeth. Though he looked like an elite reptilian predator, Ernest perceived no hint of hostility from the being, he was merely a normal merchant performing his day-to-day routine.

To avoid staring rudely at the merchant, Ernest looked around. It seemed like a typical market, with a multitude of merchants selling food, clothing, eating utensils, or various household items. He looked back to Piv, wondering if they were getting breakfast. From somewhere, Piv pulled out a sack of money.

Instead of the expected gold or silver coins, the bag held... glass marbles? She asked for several foods he didn't recognize, some *curlequins*, *ikits*, and two cups of *svarsl*. Piv paid the merchant with a small, yellow-striped cat's eye marble and several leaf-green orbs. In return, he gave her the food. These were revealed respectively as some strange-looking flowers, a small cloth pouch of something like golf ball-sized raspberries, and a couple of wooden cups of yogurt. If yogurt had the same color and smell of black coffee. Which, in a certain way, made sense for an alternate universe.

After taking their food to a nearby park, Piv pointed to Ernest's hand. "That ring, the Eye of the Beholder, is 'enchanted' to allow special abilities with its use. Though here we call it effected, referring to how its active or passive properties are permanently altered. This particular effectment is deeply enmeshed with the perception of your conscious and subconscious. The three abilities it bestows are—intangibility, invisibility, and teleportation."

She approached a picnic table, which had a space obviously designed for the shape and size of her spider's chassis. Piv handed Ernest a fork and knife. "Eat your curlequins while I continue explaining the ring's abilities."

The breakfast surprised him because the curlequin "flowers" turned out to be roasted beef. At least they had the taste and chewiness of beef, but looked exactly like soft red flowers. Ernest's earlier assumption of the svarsl was correct; it looked, smelled, and tasted like sweetened black coffee but spooned up like yogurt. The red fruit was... where was it? Misplaced?

Before he could ask about the ikits, Piv began describing the Eye. "Because the ring relies so heavily on your perception, its abilities are activated by either a reaction to certain stimuli or concentrating your intent. To start, you must recall or experience something that would prompt each ability by reflex. For intangibility, any memory of being mortally frightened of injury should suffice. The more extreme the experience, the more likely you will achieve intangibility."

Ernest searched his memories and found an appropriate one.

"Yes," he said reluctantly. "I—I... um, yes I do remember something. The day I nearly died."

Piv nodded. "That should be more than adequate. Please describe it in detail."

Ernest recalled, "This memory was so intense, everything seems indelibly imprinted. As if *every* time, I relive being nine years old again." He grew a bit nostalgic as he continued. "The neighborhood where I grew up was poor, but it still had diversions aplenty for the average young boy. We didn't have a backyard, but that was fine.

Just across the gravel road alleyway was a huge field. It was bigger than a city block, home to wildflowers, garter snakes, and the squirrels living in the old cherry tree. Once, I actually managed to catch one with my bare hands in the silly idea that I could keep it as a pet. That lasted about ten seconds; then I had to cope with a bloody thumb. I suppose I should feel lucky I didn't get rabies.

"I must have been blessed with a great deal of luck, considering all the trouble I got into. My Mom always said I was like 'Dennis the Menace.' Of course, I didn't know what she meant at the time. Next to the field, was the railroad's side-yard, used for storing train cars awaiting repair or overflow when the main yard was full. Usually, a train of fifty or more cars would sit around for several weeks or longer. I enjoyed many long days climbing up and down on the freight cars' ladders, playing hobo or acrobat. The chunks of fool's gold I found in a forgotten pile seemed like a treasure for a nine year old. The mounds of rusted scrap iron blended their dust with the orange of my hair. Needless to say, it was easy to find adventure.

"That afternoon, I was relaxing underneath one of those trains, my head resting against the solid-cast steel of the wheel axle. I had brought along a small lunch and one of my father's *Hardy Boys* books. I admit he might have been upset if he knew, but all I really wanted was a bit of adventure, and I always returned the books. After reading the fourth chapter, I heard rumbling noises. Stuff like that was pretty common in the railyard, and it wasn't obvious.

"But as I continued reading, I felt a bump against the back of my head. The axle was pushing against me! I stared in shock as it slowly rolled over. Because I sat between the rails, the wheels didn't cut me in two, but every train car was supported on either end by sets of *two* axles. I couldn't get up because the second one of these was moving toward me. I needed to remain in the gap between the rails and to duck. After the wheel truck passed, I tried getting out between the cars but was knocked back down by the brake lines' air hoses. Then I looked behind to see the wheels of another rail car rolling at me!

"At the start, I was paralyzed by shock while the wheels' axles rolled over. The cars were picking up speed. Even though it was dangerous, ironically, staying between the rails was safer... for now. As more steel moved faster above, I remembered the car at the end. These always had their brake's air hose dangling in the trackbed and would hit me too. If it was moving through that trackbed fast enough, it would break bones, or *worse*.

"I ducked again as the second car finished passing over and quickly glanced underneath the third car. Though the train was only moving five to seven miles per hour at the moment, it was still thousands of tons of steel moving around and above me. There were metal parts hanging down, so I might only get hit and knocked out, but if my hand or body was on the rail, the wheels would slice through me without slowing down at all. By the time the last car got to me, it might be moving at thirty or forty mph."

"I decided the only way out was moving right *now*, before the train moved too fast. I concentrated, watching the gap, closed my eyes and jumped—"

"There!" Piv shouted. "Concentrate on that feeling!"

Ernest stared at her. "What? What do you mean?"

"Concentrate on your memory of jumping between the train's wheels and look at the ring!"

Ernest looked down at his hand. A red light flickered in the depths of the large red stone, fading a little each time it blinked.

"It's governed by your reflexive instinct to avoid being struck," Piv said. "Since it's integrated with your reflexes, then for now, only your reflexes will automatically trigger it. The more you train for that sensation, concentrating on that desire, the more easily you'll pass through objects at will. Can you close your eyes and remember it again?"

He did so, concentrating intently, unaware the ring's light reappeared. Piv silently pulled out one of the ikits she purchased earlier.

"Open your eyes!" Just as she called out, Piv threw the red fruit.

Ernest looked in time to see it hurtling towards him! He dodged, but not fast enough. "Hey!" he yelled. "Stop that!"

"Why, human?" Piv retorted playfully. "The ikit never struck you."

"Yes, it..." Ernest started to shout, then realized she was right. He never felt it strike, even though he was sure he hadn't dodged fast enough. The fruit's pulp was a reddish smear trickling down the wall behind him. Staring at the fruit's remains, he listened as Piv explained.

"You recalled your trauma of possible injury and reflexively responded to the thrown fruit. Though this experience was different than your memory of the train, you reacted with the *same* reaction to an unwanted strike."

Ernest looked back at Piv, watching as she casually tossed another fruit up and down. Despite her projected aloofness, her next comment was amused. "Tell me, Ernest, in Earth's comedy genre of 'slapstick,' what does a character do when they have a custard cream pie?"

"You're not holding a pie," Ernest said quickly. "That's—"

"Assume it's a substitute. What does a slapstick character do with a soft, creamy object like this fruit? You know there's only one correct answer..."

Ernest cringed. "They throw it?"

Grinning broadly, Piv threw the fruit. Ernest shut his eyes and again felt nothing.

Glaring at his metallic escort, he asked, "How does this help me with phasing through objects at will?"

Piv nodded. "I'm glad you asked it that way. I deliberately pointed out the fruit and suggested I'd throw it. You need to understand on a conscious level... that the ring's ability is always there, in the background of your reflexes. These are like your lungs, in the sense that breathing is both something you can choose *and* is automatic. Your brain is always able to use this response to control your 'phasing' as you put it. When you've experienced this reflex enough with the ring, the intention of it will become the only thing you will need—to concentrate on your desire and memory of 'phasing.' The more experience you have with that, the more you can choose it."

Ernest still glared. "Without having to remember being run over by a freight train? Or getting fruit thrown at me?"

"Yes," Piv confirmed, looking at Ernest expectantly.

The moment dragged on.

"Yes?" Ernest grumbled.

Piv deadpanned, "I already told you, no need to remember the train or—"

"Unngh," Ernest groaned as he pulled loosely at his hair. "No, I meant... there was more to understanding this ring than just one ability, right? Umm... invisibility and... teleporting?"

"Perhaps. Life and death are strong motivators. Have you ever been confronted by a situation so distressing you wanted to completely disappear? Concentrate as much as possible on that memory, to the exclusion of other distractions. As with phasing, you now know how important desire, emotion and faith are to the process. These provide the drive, while a disciplined perception provides the precision."

Ernest asked, "Precision? What's that got to do with it?"

"Perception is a big part of magic," Piv answered patiently. "The foundation of magic starts with the mastery of your senses. You must not allow your environment to distract you or encourage doubt because the more you do, the less you'll be able to use magic. For invisibility, concentrate on your memory and ignore the market's noise."

Ernest closed his eyes, doing his best to push out the distractions, and concentrated on the second grade. "In school, I was basically the same innocently naïve boy who got into mischief without meaning to. We usually behaved ourselves, but for the class spelling bee, we had special reason to focus. Whoever won would represent their class against the rest of the school, and maybe even compete in nationals. After about an hour, it came down to me and Robert Deerman. The teacher gave him the word *banana*, and he slowly managed it. I got *book*. One of the easiest, even for a second grader. I wondered what the school's competition would be like and if I might go to the state championship."

"I remember..." Ernest closed his eyes, "I remember how Mrs. Birch handed me the microphone, and I spelled it out."

Ernest imagined himself at that age, standing in front of the class with everyone watching him. It felt so real, as if he was actually there again.

"B-O-O-K. *Great Expectations* is my favorite book. Book." Ernest didn't know it, but his voice was growing anxious. "Before I even finished, some of the kids started to snicker. Especially Betty Gouthe. She seemed to enjoy taunting me especially. This time she was smugger than usual."

"Ernest," Mrs. Birch asked again, "can you please repeat and spell that out?"

Ernest frowned and repeated. "B-O-O-K. There are many good stories in a book. Book."

The teacher shook her head, "No, Ernest. You didn't spell it right. Robert?"

He said, "B-O-O-K. The book was very thick and dusty. Book."

"Hey!" Ernest protested. "That's what I said!"

"No." Mrs. Birch said, "You spelled 'B-O-K.' You dropped the second 'O.' Robert, you now have the word *always*."

Robert smirked. "A-L-W-A-Y-S. The summer is always sunny here. Always."

"Good. Robert, you will represent our class for the school. Ernest, go back to your seat."

Ernest was embarrassed and angry. Book was such an easy word! He was sure he had it right. How could they not have heard the second O? His face was apple-red as he slumped into his chair.

"Bok, huh?" Betty laughed. "Is that a super-short book? Like one of your dumb comic books? Or maybe *you're* just dumb?"

His other classmates laughed, but Ernest refused to give up. "I *said* the second O! The stupid microphone wasn't close enough or something! I—"

Betty laughed again. "Stop with the lame excuses! You spelled wrong and you know it. Or are you getting upset at *losing* because you're as dumb as you look?"

"No!" Ernest screamed at her and ran from the class-room, wishing with all his heart to disappear.

Ernest stopped speaking when he realized he could see the marketplace, even though his eyes were closed. He saw it *through* his eyelids. Were they completely transparent? He raised his hand or thought he did. He couldn't see it or *any* part of himself. Apparently, the invisibility affected his entire body!

"Piv?" Ernest asked, worried. "If this is invisibility, why can't I see myself?"

"Why would you?" Piv answered. "This effect doesn't change your perception of light, only your body's property of light. Without getting too scientifically detailed, we see objects because light strikes them and reflects off. The quantum interaction of this reflecting light produces the light you're able to see. Since that interaction isn't happening, your body stops emitting a visual signal. Instead, light passes through your entire body. The ring does this for both invisibility and intangibility. It affects your body's quarks. Now, keep talking. Count or say anything sequentially. We need to make sure you understand something, so you don't hurt yourself if you have a good reason to hide."

That sounded unpleasant. "What do you mean, *hurt myself*?"

"Keep talking. I must locate your exact position," Piv said. "This will not hurt, but it may shock you."

Still concerned, Ernest counted off. He watched apprehensively as Piv got closer, tracking his voice. When he reached forty-two, the thunclik grabbed his arm. Ernest yelped as a strong tingling sensation coursed through his arm immediately. It was the same "fallen asleep" of low blood circulation, as if he'd laid down in the wrong spot.

She noted his reaction. "Yes, that's what I was referring to. If you have good reason to hide from a dangerous enemy like a knifetooth host, then you don't want to give yourself away by crying out in shock. Concentrate on desiring attention again, and you will become visible."

Ernest did, and his hand "faded in." He remembered there was still one more special ability of the ring to test. Given what these abilities needed for activating, Ernest almost dreaded the next one.

Instead, Piv simply handed him the last fruit she held. This puzzled the young human. It didn't feel like the kind of activation he was expecting. He stared at it.

"Okay, what now?"

"You can eat it if you'd like. Perfectly safe and edible for humans."

Ernest took a bite. The red fruit tasted intensely like cherry, but the pulp had the consistency of a kiwi. As he chewed, he asked, "Oruaural told me this ring also grants teleportation. I've never felt like I needed to instantly pop from place to place. Is Oruaural going to test me himself?"

"Perhaps..." Piv said slyly. "Say, what's that up there?"

He looked where she pointed. On a nearby building roof, he saw a vague figure playfully skipping like a... child? He couldn't be sure because of the distance; he could only see them because of a large, white illuminated tower behind. Ernest felt alarmed because the child skipped along the edge of a 150-foot fall.

"Piv!" Ernest said urgently, "it looks like there's a child running up there!"

"Yes," she agreed, pulling out binoculars, which she handed to Ernest. "My crystal-lensed eyes are zooming in on what looks like a young Quastran girl running dangerously close to the roof's edge. You can see her easily enough with these."

Using the binoculars, he confirmed the figure was indeed one of those crab-like people. Even with no way to compare her size, she did look smaller than the other Quastrans. He couldn't be sure if the girl was even aware of the danger. She pranced gaily about like a deer next to a drop that was *certainly* lethal for any human.

"We've got to do something!" Ernest cried.

"What would that be?" Piv calmly replied. "We're down here. She's up there. We have no way to get up to her, nor do we have any way to intervene from down here. Worrying about something I can do nothing about is unproductive."

Galled by her unconcern, Ernest shouted, "We can still yell up to her, or call for help!"

His heart skipped a bit when he saw the girl stop suddenly and teeter on the edge. Abruptly, the perspective changed, as if he was standing inches away from a wall. Dropping the binoculars, Ernest realized that his position *had* changed, and he was standing on the roof. He looked around and saw the crab-girl laughing merrily at her parkour.

Ernest shouted, "Get away from there!"

The Quastran seemed oblivious, giggling in response. He decided this was not a time for thinking, but for *action*. Ernest threw himself toward the crustacean girl and pulled her away from the edge. He took a deep breath as the girl laughed uncontrollably, which only added to his frustration and confusion.

"What's wrong with you?" Ernest demanded. "You could have fallen to your death!"

"Oh relax, *mortal*," the girl chuckled. "There was never any danger; you only *thought* there was."

From the start, the encounter felt odd, but now the girl's tone as she said "mortal" bothered Ernest especially. She was out of place because even in an interdimensional insane asylum, how often did children scamper along roof edges? Her saying "mortal" *that* way suggested...

No, Ernest assured his thoughts, *that can't be right, Oruaural is a–*

"Human man?" the strange girl finished. "Or maybe *this!*" She began growing, her body changing shape, the crab's chitinous exoskeleton becoming a *new* form.

"No," Ernest groaned with his head in hands. "No! That is *not* right!"

Rapidly, the figure grew taller, with Vungir bat wings spreading out, covered in fine fur. If this was Oruaural, she appeared as a svelte-furred *woman*. Somehow, her child-sized clothes had adjusted to the changing body without tearing as they stretched.

"*Exactly* right, mortal!" Oruaural wore a huge grin on "her" face. "As you should already know, Oruaural loves surprises, especially if the surprise *is* Oruaural! Hahahahahahahahahahahaha!"

Ernest groaned again, though quieter than before. Even if the joke was on him, he had to admit it was funny. He was confused why the madly powerful Emissary would use this form. Though that was clearly a question for after Oruaural finished laughing.

"Ah, haha, hoom hoom," Oruaural uttered, either clearing her throat or still chuckling. "Heheh... so anyway, now you know how the ring's teleportation works. Remember, you needed to feel strongly about something, and you reacted exactly as you should have. Be proud of that—many are less caring than you. Shouldn't you be getting back down to Piv now?"

"Yes?"

"Since you teleported up here, how do you get back down?"

"Uh..." Ernest walked to the edge and saw Piv, merrily waving back from the ground.

"Mwah!" Oruaural suddenly shouted behind him.

Before he had any time to even *think* about what that was, Ernest was thrown off the roof. As he realized he was falling toward the ground, his perspective suddenly changed again, to about five feet away from crashing. Though his position in falling had changed, the velocity he had at the point of his fall, had *not* changed. This caused him to collide hard with the ground, sprawling forward by fifteen feet, and flailing his limbs. Ernest groaned again but for a very *different* reason than before. Piv helped him up, brushing him off as she did so, and handed him a cup of water.

After recovering, Ernest demanded, "What the hell was that?"

Oruaural answered him by erupting blithely from the ground. "Well, that should be obvious. Oruaural shouted, blasting you off the roof. After finding yourself violently thrown into the air, you naturally had another powerful emotion, wanting *very* much to be safe. So *obviously*, you teleported yourself to safety. Then Oruaural burst out of the ground like a mushroom!"

"Not cool!"

Oruaural frowned. "But Ernest, of course it is!"

"*What?*"

"You told me—later in your timeline but earlier in mine—how you *love* mushrooms!"

"No, getting blasted off the roof! I could have *died*!"

Oruaural rolled her eyes. "Oruaural knew you were not in any danger, because Oruaural already knows a full timeline of the Shifting Stones and of Oruaural. So Oruaural already knew you wouldn't be hurt. You are a *main character*, after all. Plus, you needed a real, serious reason to test teleportation. Like the other abilities, the more you use it, the easier it will get, like learning to ride a bicycle! And yes, we *are* using the 'training wheels.'"

Squeamish about what *no* "training wheels" would be like, Ernest changed the subject. "You know what? Let's not practice using the ring right now. I—I don't think I... I'm worn out. I need some rest. Um... I'm curious— you approached me before as a male. Why appear as a female now?"

"Oh, you silly human!" Oruaural laughed loudly, her wings rippling as she rocked back and forth. "Because that man you met *was* Oruaural. Therefore, it was *not* me! *I* am always female because it's what I am, as Oruaural. Now, of course Oruaural knows you don't understand this, but your acceptance feast hasn't been celebrated yet. Don't worry, that's next! It's being merged with the

Restoration Ceremony. Oh, and before you ask, that giant ribbon of farmland behind you is *exactly* what it looks like—a giant ribbon of farmland."

Ernest spun around to see what Oruaural described on the horizon's edge. Like a massively larger version of a crescent moon, a ribbon stretched from one side of the horizon to the other in the black sky. Like all the floating landmasses, the swathe was well lit even with no sun. This allowed Ernest to easily see that the circular shape did appear to be a massive ribbon of farmland, like a planetary ring of solid land surrounding the sphere on which he stood.

Ernest tried to comprehend it. "Oruaural, why didn't you tell me about this before?"

There was no response.

"Oruaural?"

Quiet.

Ernest turned around and saw only Piv, relaxing on her arachnid chassis.

"Where's Oruaural?"

Piv answered matter-of-factly. "Waiting for us at the feast, of course. Oruaural wanted to make sure you saw the Iris before we went back inside. Come along now, they're all waiting for us."

"Wait." Ernest lingered. "Didn't Oruaural call this city Delirium?"

"Yes," Piv agreed, as if he were a precocious child. "Now, aren't you coming?"

Ernest persisted. "Then what's this Iris you're talking about?"

Piv halted abruptly, her back venting steam as though irritated. "We *just* pointed it out, but I suppose I must be specific. Turn around."

Ernest turned and had a more open view of the broadly curving ribbon of farmland. Piv walked up next to him so he could clearly see where her bronze metallic arm pointed.

"That," she said, "is the Iris. It is a large circular disc of solid land surrounding the Pupil, the sphere on which we stand. The *combination* of the two is the capitol of the Shifting Stones, named Delirium. The Pupil never moves, unlike the Iris. Although never leaving the Pupil, the Iris spins, tilts or swirls perpetually around the sphere. This motion regulates the large bodies of water on the Iris, but the rivers and tides here behave much differently than Earth's. Now, do you want to focus on more details or to go on to the acceptance celebrations? The feast is being held in your honor for agreeing to record this story, after all."

Ernest still didn't know how he felt about an obligation he was apparently already doing, but an acceptance feast felt somehow unnecessary. After all he'd seen so far, he wasn't sure if he should be flattered or anxious.

Ernest and Piv walked back to Oruaural's palace and stood at a pair of tall doors. These revealed a formal dining hall so cavernous it resembled a cathedral's interior. But Oruaural must have felt a cathedral's interior wasn't big enough, because the dining hall was so expansive that he couldn't see the other side. If not for the implied presence of a roof, he might've wondered if it was a room at all. Above, there was only the indoor haze of dim lighting and dust. The huge columns clearly supported something, though they appeared more like massive redwood trees than manmade columns.

Interspersed among the columns were *thousands* of Shifting Stones residents, as if the entire city had filled in for the biggest banquet imaginable. They varied as much as their number permitted—crab-like Quastrans, bat-winged Vungir, hornet-like Thvenel, serpentine Tasdo, and the Aejlii, their forms combining cat with fish. All the different races were represented, but they also varied among their own kind. Fat and thin, stocky and lanky, short and tall, hyperactive and dozing, chatty and quiet— more variety than anyone could describe. Some even appeared to be burping or behaving rudely in other ways, such as localized food fights. But no one seemed angry or willing to violently fight each other.

Without any explanation for why, some distant tables were empty, but they were indicated as reserved. The room's size stretched beyond the limits of Ernest's vision. He was surprised that he could still *be* surprised, yet he was.

Then he heard an amused chuckling and spun around.

Oruaural was there, appearing as the bat-like Vungir woman he saw before. Now she wore a shimmering egg-plant purple and gold gown that appeared as if its fabric were literally made of tiny gemstones. Gold egg-shaped earrings, each the size of a baseball, shone from the large fox-shaped ears above her head.

"Mortals are easily overwhelmed, but it's a natural reaction, so Oruaural will not make fun. Oruaural felt you'd want the preparation of entering from the doors, rather than teleporting into the middle of it. Anyway, having done that—"

Oruaural laid a hand on Ernest's shoulder, and suddenly they were surrounded by the throng. Oruaural paused, then flapped her bat wings and rose gently into the air.

She launched into a speech with a grandly projecting tone. "Mad Legions of the Shifting Stones! All who seek understanding or comfort for yourselves and those affected by your disorders! This sanctuary is a place to find yourselves, and to heal. After your pain has resolved, life and love can begin anew. Oruaural assumes the responsibility of providing care and sanctuary. Even to the best interests of returning you to your loved ones, if wished.

"The responsibility of life is to pursue its own expression, to test itself constantly and defy its odds. For Oruaural, this has become a crusade to protect those for whom life no longer makes sense. Our great creator Ekallr gave us definitions of righteousness in the Edicts of Life. You must have sanctuary from your mental afflictions to find sanity again.

"Spirit leads our decisions and our actions, for it dwells within the body, and our spirits are strengthened by sharing stories. Like a seed growing into a majestic tree, faith can motivate us to mighty deeds and inspires actions against the odds. For this, the Shifting Stones needs someone to share your stories where you cannot go.

Oruaural presents to you the Scribe and Court Librarian, Ernest Redsmith!"

As Oruaural bellowed this to the roaring crowd, Ernest found himself rising high into the air on a brightly lit pedestal. He felt exposed and terribly embarrassed. Without realizing it, Ernest used the ring to disappear.

"Come now, Ernie," Oruaural clucked. "This is why Piv guided you to the doors first! Do you mind if Oruaural shortens your name to Ernie? It's easier, even if you're not with Bert or singing about rubber duckies!"

Oruaural paused long enough for Ernest to take a steadying breath. He expected the insane... whatever she wanted to call herself, to give him time to answer, at least. No such luck.

"Of course you hate the idea of being called Ernie!" Instead of sympathy, she was jovial. "Though I can't imagine why you'd hate that—he's the funnier of those two. We have our own versions of Big Bird here. You could say we ride them, too, but they're *not* chocobos. Anyhoo, Oruaural will keep calling you Ernest, if you'd prefer. Oruaural could have teleported your here without warning, but that's disrespectful. There are special reasons to *not* teleport you. Surely, you'd have not wanted to *pee* on the other guests if you're the guest of honor. But if you're Oruaural's guest, does that mean Oruaural *is* honor? Ah, don't answer, perhaps it's better to say it *that* way."

Addressing Ernest's reaction, she told the crowd, "Don't worry, he's just a bit shy. You're *not* having a hallucination... well, probably not *all* of you, anyway. Oruaural's also happy to address those residents who have recovered. Before they leave us, we should pray that their loved ones welcome them again."

As she said this, many bowed their heads solemnly. Everyone fell respectfully quiet. Then from the vicinity of the double doors, a large group of people walked up, varying in appearance as much as the massive crowd, but they seemed different. Calmer, cleaner, and composed. Not that the first crowd lacked cleanliness or calm individuals, but none of this group was messy or misbehaving at all. The entire new group looked completely sane.

After the respectful quiet—apparently for the newcomers—Oruaural continued. "Children of Aerth, although Oruaural regrets your leaving our sanctuary, Oruaural feels overjoyed you can return to your friends and families and mend your damaged relationships. Go now, with our blessing and wishes for your lives to be happier."

The crowd roared again, even louder. The new group sat down at the reserved tables and began chatting together.

"Are you having a good time?" Oruaural asked Ernest.

Ernest blinked, processing what just happened. One moment, he was high up on the pedestal, the next he was comfortably sitting at one of the reserved tables, holding a fork speared into some kind of strange-looking pasta. Like the massive bat she resembled now, Oruaural hung upside down, resting on a hooked stand. Their new positions placed her next to Ernest. Another Vungir hung in the same way next to her, this one was a muscular male with reddish fur, making the Vungir look even more vulpine.

The sudden change in perspective slowed his response, but Ernest asked the obvious. "What?"

She repeated herself after swallowing a frosted tart. "Are you having a good time?"

"Yes," Ernest began cautiously, unsure of how to continue. "I'm not complaining, but why are you celebrating my acceptance? Also, I understand why you met me under the guise of another human—you didn't want to frighten me. But why appear as a man and then as a woman? It's easier to keep track if you're not changing so much."

"But we did meet," the Vungir man said. "I'm Oruaural, remember?"

Again confused, Ernest pointed to the Vungir woman. "She isn't?"

"Of course, she is," he said casually. "I'm Oruaural just as much as she is."

Ernest stared.

"To make it easier," the lady said, "try thinking of Oruaural as 'two-in-one.' I am a woman, and he is a man, but we are the same person. Sort of. As a woman, there are *specific* differences in detail from my male aspect, but—"

"I am still Oruaural." The gentleman completed his lady's statement seamlessly. "If it's easier, Oruaural's male form is always 'Oru,' and Oruaural's female form is always 'Aural.' Despite how Oruaural changes form, Oruaural's gender *never* changes."

Ernest thought quietly, then asked, "One person, two bodies?"

"Yes!" they said in stereo. "Oruaural's thoughts and feelings are so completely linked between Oruaural's bodies, that Oruaural is *one* person. This story's audience has a naturally different perspective of this, having never experienced combined personhood. If it's easier for you, try thinking of Oruaural as just 'Oru' and or 'Aural.' Sometimes, people may even refer to Oruaural as 'Oru-Aural.'"

Piv broke her silence. "Although most of the Emissaries are able to shapeshift, as one of the strongest Ptiris, the Emissary of Madness is different. Individually, Oru and Aural are weaker than any other Emissary. But married together, they are stronger and often synchronize completely. Their combined power outperforms nearly all the others, short of the great creator himself, Ekallr."

"Yes!" Oru and Aural cried happily. "Oruaural fears nothing. Well, there is something, but not in a bad way. Enough of that, this feast is not meant to celebrate Oruaural!"

Aural tossed Ernest a fruit, which he recalled with a chagrin, was the same kind Piv threw at him earlier.

Excitedly she said "Later, you're going to join Hahn and Laeljah! You don't know them yet, but you will. As this story's teller, your most important purpose is to *tell* it. Hahn and Laeljah *are* the story, but this feast is now. So, enjoy yourself before the party crashers come to spill blood for their confetti!"

Ernest took a bite of his fruit, then coughed a little. "Party crashers? *Blood*? What—"

An awful noise tore through the dining hall. It sounded like tortured metal and wooden beams ripping apart, combining into the crash of thunder. Shattering the calm as surely as the noise, a huge hole into darkness or... *nothingness* appeared. A moment later, a screaming horde of dark warriors came pouring out, attacking with savage ruthlessness.

The metallic thunclik fought back, with some of the diners joining them. The defenders used a variety of weapons—swords, clubs, axes, and crossbows. The crossbow bolts seemed as effective in puncturing the warriors' armor, as bullets. The invaders favored ranged-fire attacks, while the defending thunclik preferred melee weapons. They were no less ferocious with their blades and maces.

Though thunclik bodies were metallic, a few were injured. Ernest expected their skin to behave like solid metal when damaged. Instead, the wounded thunclik he saw were clearly flesh and blood—*metal* flesh and blood. Their injuries spilled droplets of a shimmering liquid. Mercury? The one wound he saw in detail—a large shoulder gash—revealed a shining metallic substance underneath what might've been a large bony plate. If it *was* bone. How did they have organic tissue made of metal? Metal wasn't flexible like tissue!

Ernest had no time to figure this out, as a wedge-shaped group of five monsters rushed at him. The most disturbing thing about these invaders wasn't the violent attacks, or that they almost looked like the *same* people who were sitting next to him only a minute ago. The most frightening thing of these monsters wasn't even their evil portal of darkness. The most frightening thing of these monsters was the way their bodies had six-inch long knife-shaped shards of... something. Ernest couldn't tell if these were knives of metal or bone, but the monsters' muscles seemed to have grown up *around* the blades. And each of the "knives" seemed to "twitch" like hellish pairings of mandibles. Interrupting the enemies' charge was a squad of four thunclik. They surrounded Ernest in a guarded formation, each with a shield like Piv's. With no apparent communication, the four raised their shields, in time to block a fierce spread of crossbow darts. Ernest realized Piv was among the four thunclik who tasked themselves with protecting him.

"Become invisible or intangible with the ring," she shouted at him, "but do *not* teleport out! We still don't know where they all are. If you teleport, you might be surrounded by the enemy. We must make our stand here!"

Then she heaved her shield against a murderous battle-ax's swing. Her black-armored opponent snarled in pain as the thunclik thrust her sword all the way through his body. Ernest realized that, like the shield, her blade appeared to grow out of Piv's arm, the limb now a hardened sword. Another thunclik on their right flank had also grown a crossbow from her arm, with a cylinder-shaped magazine of deadly bolts. The few darts Ernest got a good look at seemed sharp enough to draw blood from mere touch, shaped as they were like bladed drill bits.

Wondering what Oru and Aural was doing about this, Ernest looked around. Only to be aghast at seeing the Emissary pair sitting in lounge chairs and... eating popcorn? They sat watching as if it was all a particularly exciting football game, laughing as the enemy fell. They even wore face-paint, gold-colored jerseys, cheese-hats, and waved giant sports fingers. Decorating these foam fingers was a symbol that suggested their peculiar unified duality, along with a large numeral one. As another squad of thunclik knocked away a surge of enemies, Oru and Aural cheered. *"Rah, rah, rah, sis-boom-bah!"*

Ernest was torn by the incredulity of it, how even in the midst of *this*, they could make him laugh. But they were also insane.

Difficult as it was for him to understand, the thunclik seemed to interlock their shields together. He briefly wondered what sort of communication they used to coordinate their movements as a team. With a terrifying bellow, one of the enemy soldiers swung something from their arm. The object reminded Ernest of a whisking boomerang, but completely silent. Ernest shouted for a thunclik, pointing out the projectile, and she watched it approach. It was so fast he could barely track it, but then he realized it was swinging toward him. The thunclik watching the weapon wasn't close enough to intercept it with her shield.

He reached for Piv, who seemed unaware of the flying weapon as she tried flinging off a grasping tentacled *thing* from one of her arachnid legs. Suddenly, without even moving her head, Piv threw up her shield in time to knock the weapon away, sending it glancing off toward a column. More enemy soldiers charged to replenish their waning numbers, but no new defenders appeared. Despite this,

the thunclik were *more* than a match for them, especially as the diners—the Mad Legions—fought alongside.
Apparently, many had brought their own weapons to the
feast, as if they'd *expected* a fight to be part of the celebration. Ernest briefly wondered if that was true, but that
didn't make any sense. Unless—

"**Kill**!" Even worse than his nightmarish pawns, a
fifty-foot tall horned giant appeared out of the smoky
darkness, roaring its bloodthirsty demand and pointing
directly at Ernest.

Turning toward him as one, the enemy attacked.

In the lead of the charge was an exceptionally large,
strong, and *vicious* brute. A monstrous Quastran, with
full-plate armor reinforcing his crab-like chitin. It seemed
to make his hide about as indestructible as it looked evil,
and it looked like pretty darn evil. He ran with all the
predatory ferocity of a lion, screaming with the fanatical zeal of a suicide bomber. Clearly, Ernest was his
only target, because he rammed straight through every
obstacle, tossing aside even his own comrades. If they
didn't move fast enough, the monster slashed them apart
with a greatsword as immensely long as he was tall.

"Shield-scale formation!" Piv shouted.

Immediately, those thunclik that could, paired up.
They interlocked their shields, fortifying a barricading
line between Ernest and the invaders. The thunclik resonated with a unifying, rhythmic ticking noise, amplified so
much it vibrated Ernest's bones. They held their shields in
front and above, like an ancient Roman shield wall.

As the thunclik marched forward, unifying their movement, they pointed their blades rigidly between the shields. As frightening as the attackers were, the thunclik defended with a force Ernest never imagined possible. Returning strength for strength, he felt maybe they'd survive after all. Unbowed, the giant bellowed his rage at their denial and galloped at them on three armored legs, raising his massive blade. Just before the berserker reached them, Piv and three other thunclik broke formation, punching the monster's chest. Their synchronized strikes sent the monster reeling backward.

"Yes!" Ernest shouted excitedly.

Tossing handfuls of sparkles into the air, Oru and Aural blew a cheer with noisemakers. But it was a short-lived feeling.

Infuriated, the enemy commander roared his anger, crashed the line toward Ernest, and lobbed a flaming spear at Piv. The weapon pierced through her chest, puncturing her arachnid-like rear. The abdomen exploded with a small burst of steam and smoke. Ignoring the severe damage, she screamed, wildly swung her blade, and leaped into the horde. Sensing the battle had turned, the enemy soldiers pressed forward, swarming over several more thunclik. The horned commander laughed harshly, charging Ernest while rapidly swinging an immense hammer.

"**Nooo!**" Oru and Aural shouted in unison.

Out of nowhere, a huge, bare foot kicked the enemy commander across the banquet hall floor and back through his dark portal of nothingness. The dark cloud quickly grew smaller, as if the portal was closing. The aggression of the horde morphed now into fear, and they fled toward the shrinking portal. The few who stood their ground were mopped up with little effort.

Even with the unpredictable and *strange* victory that literally kicked out the commander, the scene's triumph was muted. Destroyed thunclik lay strewn about, venting smoke and steam. Piv's broken body lay on the floor, crystalline eyes now dark and cracked. The tip of her shattered sword was stuck in a dead enemy's chest. The now lifeless solid metal legs had skewered several more enemy bodies before stopping.

She fought to the last with everything she had.

Quadrant Three:

The Various Natures of Focus

Do you have faith? Or doubt? Sometimes the eyes of the spirit are led true, and sometimes not. Seek to understand fully what your spirit sees, and this will uplift your body.

Faith without action is spirit without life.

Action without faith is life without spirit.

– The Unknown Prophet, possibly during Agnok

E rnest stared at the carnage and destruction surrounding him. The broken bodies of the dead and maimed were *awful*. Because they were scattered all around, he couldn't avoid seeing them. The thunclik busied themselves with the casualties. It was surreal—a multitude gathered in joyous celebration was now a vicious battle's devastation. Witnessing the scene change so suddenly from one extreme to its complete polar opposite was such a shock Ernest didn't know how to handle it.

He expected Oru and Aural to be despondent or angry, or some emotion he felt himself. They certainly seemed angry when they stomped the battle to an end.

"Ernest!" Oru called as he gently glided over on his bat wings. "Now that those rude guests have been ejected—"

"Rude?" Ernest gaped. "Guests? They tried to kill us all! Why aren't you more upset?"

Oru seemed remarkably sane for the moment, which disturbed him even more. All he had seen of Oru and... Aural, was insanity. Although the mad Emissary had never been directly hostile with Ernest, seeing him this out of character disturbed him.

"Calm down," Oru said. "Of course, they tried to kill everyone and especially targeted you. But they weren't successful, were they?"

Ernest tried to speak, but Oru talked over him.

"Oruaural has admittedly been cryptic about this, but the cat is out of the bag now. Besides, what's the point in putting cats in bags? Cats *love* bags! They happily snuggle in on their own! In their aloofness, they don't need any fancy—shmancy beds! What was Oru talking about? The partycrashers, of course! Oruaural's power ensures *complete* awareness of everything that happens in the timeline of Oruaural's past, present, and future, including what just happened here. Oruaural saw it coming and was prepared. This extends to a similar awareness of the Shifting Stones. With this, Oruaural will help you on your coming adventure. To fight something that is certain to happen means it can't be *stopped* from happening. You can only *prepare* for how you will react to it, including how to stop it from getting worse, or even stopping the threat completely."

"Yes," Ernest persisted, "but you could have changed your feast, or had your guards—"

"Then the enemy would attack at some other time and perhaps change their tactics. The COBWEB's quantum entanglement superluminal frequency connection is instantaneously fast, but the thunclik can only react to most events as they happen, not before. But the reaction time is always able to stop the rebellious Emissaries from holding anyplace here for long. Their personal best has only been ten minutes! Bu' Zast is rather single-mindedly stupid that way. He knows **he** can't win but tries regardless. But Oruaural is never unprepared."

Ernest's eyes widened. "That horror you kicked out was—"

Oru laughed, resuming his previous bearing. "*Him*? Oh dear, no! That was one of his higher-level lieutenants. If Bu' Zast *could* come here, you'd know the difference! That bunch of black-armored-post-nuclear-apocalypse rejects was only a *part* of his army. Right now, we are doing something about them. See?"

He pointed to groups of thunclik and various survivors. A few people cried with shock, or rested their injuries. But most wore expressions of grim satisfaction, as if the battle was one of the most enjoyable experiences of their lives. Of all these, Ernest noticed more than he expected, had survived. He noted most of the defenders' bodies were picked up now, loaded into carts parked nearby. All the severely injured thunclik were gone.

Without a chance to see the injured thunclik, Ernest decided to get a better look at the enemy bodies. He didn't have much time during the battle, but noticed more clearly now, these were monstrously distorted versions of the people he'd met here. At first, he thought they all had severe wounds. On closer inspection, the wounds were *not* inflicted in the battle, but were actually pincers jutting out from corrupted flesh.

Ernest tried reaching for one to look closer. Oru startled him by pulling him away quickly. "Hold up there. Don't touch those!"

Anticipating the question, Oru said, "They're Knifetooth hosts. The pincers you were about to grab are the teeth of the parasites. If they get inside a host, they drastically mutate the flesh around the parasite. The host becomes stronger and tougher. They also become more aggressive and violent as they acquiesce to their darker emotions. Often, the hosts will allow multiple parasites to live inside their bodies to turn themselves into brutish monsters. Lusting for power, some seek to become hosts; some hosts have it forced against them. The thunclik will do what they can to remove and kill the parasites. For now, the surviving hosts will be kept at Oruaural's prison stone, Gakbah. When they've demonstrated a true willingness to live in peace with others, they will be released. We can't permit chaos and unrestrained violence. This may feel like a strange contradiction of order in a land of madness, but allowing anarchy destroys peace. We shouldn't waste more time on knifetooth. We need to be going so you can rejoin Piv. She can tell you more about them herself."

Ernest stared a bit more at the monster. The knife-tooth host looked like a combination of a werewolf, vampire, and a zombie with a scattering of equally monstrous insectoid pincers poking out. Oru's comment registered with Ernest as the Emissary urged him along.

"Piv? Wasn't she destroyed in the battle?" Ernest asked.

"Yes, she was. That's why we have to go find her."

Ernest persisted. "Won't you at least tell me what th—"

Oru halted. "No, Oru doesn't have to tell you what that means if you're going to see it anyway. You'll need to be shown where it is for later, when you teleport with the ring. So Oru will take you back to Aural."

After returning back to Aural, Oru rubbed his pointed snout against his wife's affectionately. Then they opened the doors into the anteroom. Hurrying through, Ernest was given no explanation. He hoped he would understand later. For now, he had to accept ignorance. At the anteroom's doors, the two Vungir grabbed him and flapped their wings. They flew just slow enough for Ernest to keep track—a sharp left, then a long straight shot down a hall. After a couple more turns, they arrived at a circular room serving as a junction. There were eight doors, including the archway they passed through.

The entire room rotated with a ticking rhythm like a gear. After they settled on the floor, Ernest felt the movement underneath him. He turned around and saw the wall tick-ticking *through* the arch. He wondered why, but didn't ask. Behind the opening they'd passed through, Ernest noted each doorframe was marked with a strange symbol. When the wall finally reached one particular door, the wall clicked with a loud sound of solid metal parts locking in place.

The door, a complex intermeshing of metal gears, opened as the metal bands slid into the sides of the doorway. Except for the arch they passed through, all the doors were like this, with geared teeth in strips of bronze metal. He briefly wondered why bronze was the metal of choice until his curiosity was caught up in staring at the room beyond. On the left, were shelves upon shelves of various metal parts. On the right, were more shelves, bearing various blue-green crystal triangular prisms, and variations of thin metal sheets. Ahead, was a countertop manned by a thunclik of a different form than Piv, or most others he had seen.

The most obvious difference, was that this one looked masculine, with broad muscular shoulders. Ernest realized all the thunclik he had seen were female, or so their faces and torsos appeared. The others all served in militaristic roles—guarding, patrolling, peacekeeping. Presumably, all had arms that could reshape into swords or crossbows. This thunclik seemed incongruous, hidden away as a clerk. Although he didn't know why, for some reason Ernest found himself expecting something else. He spent so much time trying to think about this, that he wasn't thinking about much else.

"Why are you here?"

The clerk's question brought Ernest back to cognizance. For all the expressions he had seen of the thunclik, Ernest understood the metallic man was clearly surprised to see someone there, but was not objecting. Behind him, were shelves of what looked like preassembled thunclik body parts—legs, arms, torsos, and others he didn't recognize—as well as pools of cable in gear assemblies, pistons, and spring-loaded mechanisms.

An aisle led to the left, another to the right, while another led straight back. To the clerk's right, one of the blue-green prisms was held in a bronze caliper array, light shining through it in several directions. A machine next to it showed a number of colored lights, symbols, and a waving line. Ernest couldn't be sure exactly what the device was, but it looked like an oscilloscope, measuring the prism's light. Surely this was a place for maintenance, repair, and assembly of thunclik mechanical parts. Though not rude, the clerk was obviously confused about Ernest's presence.

"Don't worry, he's with *me*," Oru and Aural said in unison. "Ernest needs to see this for the benefit of other mortals. Lead the way to the corpus fusion chambers."

This startled the bronze man, but he didn't argue. "Er, yes, Oruaural. Please forgive your servant for not understanding. He is allowed to see the other areas then?"

The peculiar sense of Oru's and Aural's unified expression continued as they nodded together. "Yes, but only what's needed. Let's move on now."

He quickly answered, "Yes, my Emissary."

Ernest wondered about the clerk's reaction. It didn't seem the right time to ask about it, so he quietly followed their lead. They went down a straight hall lined with doors, all of which were ordinary wood rather than bronze. At the end of the hall, another room opened up ahead with a 90 degree left turn. It was connected by a doorway to the clerk's desk and surrounded by more of the complicated equipment. On the other side, was a row of connected metal chambers. Each had a control console with buttons, dials, switches, more display screens, and a viewing window. There were also handles for manual adjustment. Inside the first chamber, Ernest saw devices that looked like lasers.

"As you have already guessed," Oru gestured, "this is where we repair or replace our thunclik. You've also noticed how the thunclik aren't all gears and pistachios. Er, that's the word humans use for nuts, isn't it? Anyway, they are *more* than nuts and bolts. They contain flesh and bone like you. Well, not *quite* like you. Yes, they have muscles, blood, nerves, and steam furnace stomachs, but it is all made of metal and inorganic stuff. Even their skin! At a microscopic level, even living cells can be made of metal. Your impression is correct—those *are* lasers in there."

Ernest looked around, initially to ask about the lasers and the male clerk. All the other thunclik he had seen so far had appeared to be female. If they reproduced as male and female, why did they need this place?

Ernest turned around to ask Oru and Aural, "I understand this place might be used to heal, or 'repair' perhaps, thunclik bodies. But it also looks like this is how thunclik reproduce. Is this why I haven't seen any thunclik children?"

The clerk's bronze skin darkened as though tarnished, and his body's posture suggested embarrassment. Apparently oblivious to this, Oru and Aural abruptly embraced each other. They licked each other's snouts with such a furious affection, it almost seemed like rage. Ernest had noticed this among the Vungir before, but only now realized now this was how they kissed. Because of their faces' shapes, Vungir couldn't kiss like humans, so they licked each other's snouts instead. But most weren't quite this... passionate. Perhaps this intensity increased the clerk's new awkwardness, or perhaps it was something else Ernest didn't understand.

"Thunclik *do* procreate." The other man answered with an uncomfortable slowness. "We start that process in... uh... a similar way to yours. But thunclik bodies develop differently. You haven't seen any of our children because we have offspring very rarely, and they hatch from eggs full-grown."

Oru and Aural broke their embrace, and Aural spoke up with a solemn tone. "It's more important for Ernest that you finish describing the rest of the reassembly process. Get the limbs and other parts ready."

"The limbs?" the clerk asked.

Ernest pointed to the clerk. "Doesn't he have a name?"

"Yes, obviously," Oru replied.

They all stood quietly staring at each other.

"Well?" Ernest asked. "Why aren't you telling me it?"

"Because," they both replied, "you haven't asked for it."

"Isn't that... uh, what I'm doing now?"

"No, you're asking why Oruaural hasn't told you his name. Which is not the same as asking *for* his name."

Ernest sighed. "Fine, what is his name?"

"Velosit. You should know that every thunclik name has a special meaning. Velosit's refers to his speed. Piv's name refers to how she's close to the center, where the story *pivots*. You could ask what this means, but I'm certain you would rather watch Velosit work. Isn't that right? Not left, or in angles of acute versus obtuse, but *correct*?"

At this prompting, Ernest noticed Velosit had disappeared. Looking further down the aisle, he saw the thunclik operating another control panel. However, his hands didn't seem to touch the panel. Velosit moved his arms and hands so fast they blurred into invisibility. Ernest walked over to get a closer look in the chamber and saw... body parts? The lasers seemed to be *shooting* at the body parts.

To say that Ernest found this morbid was an understatement. He imagined a body had been torn apart and the lasers focusing—

"Naturally," Oru interrupted, "you're thinking we've torn apart a thunclik. Goriness with a laser light show! Laughable, but that's not what this is. Oruaural reminds you the thunclik are made primarily of various metals, even their flesh and blood! This means their bodies can be healed by precision welding lasers."

"These lasers" Aural continued, "apply ionized particles from gas oxides of those metals in the chamber, by crossing the laser streams. But instead of capturing a giant demonic ghostie, we're laser-welding all the metallic flesh to 3-D print new thunclik tissue. Even new body parts, if needed."

Midway through the commentary, Ernest looked up to stare at Oru and Aural as they chatted. Their speech seamlessly flowed from one into the other. But this only highlighted the sense of them as "two-in-one." Fortunately, he was paying attention when Oruaural described lasers that 3-D printed metallic flesh. So, Ernest only needed it explained twice.

Seeing the reconstruction of the thunclik head, confirmed this *was* Piv being brought back. Velosit had already moved down twenty-four more chambers after only a half-hour. The thunclik man was fast, but Ernest had no comparison for restoring a creature made of living metal. Currently, he was seeing those dark, blue-green crystals being placed precisely in the metallic skull.

"What are those?"

Aural answered, "Her brain."

Ernest wondered aloud. "Crystals for brains?"

"Yes." Oru nodded "There are two kinds of magnets on Earth, monopoles and dipoles. The dipoles are the ones you're more familiar with, the ones with positive and negative. Not to say they're optimists or pessimists, because magnets don't have emotions. These crystals have magnetic fields, too."

Oru and Aural each held up a single hand with a triangular crystal. When they brought the crystals near each other at specific corners, they pulled at each other like magnets. Turning them showed obvious repulsion. However, when turned to the *third* corner, they floated next to each other. The display was astounding, like so much else in this odd world, and reminded Ernest of something.

"Is that why your stones 'shift?'" Ernest asked. "Why they're floating and drifting around?"

"It is," Oru and Aural said. "These crystals are not monopoles, with only one magnetic charge, or dipoles, with two. These are *tri*poles. The third pole is the combination of both attraction *and* repulsion. Of course, Oruaural has amplified these crystals' magnetic fields for display. Alone, the charges merely regulate the electrical pulse that passes through the crystal. This means each prism has the capability of processing electrical pulses like Earth's typical computers. Oruaural is flattered your scientists are dancing around with quantum computing and would love to see them try swing! Though you'd probably need to have a great deal of stamina to throw your dancing partner up in the air, and scientists seem to exercise their intellect more than their bodies.

"Anyhoo, the amusing parts of quantum computing are qubits. *Both* are 0 and 1. Like Oruaural. The third magnetic pole is the same in that sense, making each crystal a qubit that can perform quantum computations without all that fancy noise suppression equipment. It would be a bit difficult for Oruaural's thunclik if their heads were the size of refrigerators! Oruaural finds it amusing that scientists on Earth *have* made these crystals but do not yet understand how to assemble them in a computational matrix. Perhaps they will after this book has been published, perhaps not. Oruaural wants our audience to enjoy being surprised."

Ernest thought about this revelation and wondered about the thunclik. Was this the secret to creating truly self-aware, even *emotional,* computerized machines? The Holy Grail of artificial intelligence? Ernest recognized in Oruaural's words that this was probably as much as the Emissary would say on the subject. At least for now.

Ernest asked. "Why has Velosit been so quiet?"

The thunclik answered for himself. "Because I must focus on my work. The slightest lapse may result in *disastrous* reconstruction of the brain."

"Yes," Oru and Aural agreed. "Velosit must concentrate, *especially* about the crystals. We will leave him and go look at the renewed arachnid power chassis."

It occurred to Ernest that he didn't see any of the arachnid chassis—this was only the torso. That detail about body parts being pre-made was sensible with metallic 3-D printing. As they left the torso, he noted it was nearly finished, though it lacked Piv's legs and the spider abdomen.

"Why is the chassis being assembled separately?"

"Because it is."

Unsatisfying as this answer was, Ernest remembered cryptic vagueness was a typical prelude to the demonstrative examples. He grumbled but followed. When they reached the chassis assembly area, he recognized something.

A pair of solid metal wheels with thick spokes were attached to a metal drum the size of a large paint bucket. Even though the wheels were small as a child's bicycle tire, the solid metal suggested *serious* weight. Two metal rods connected to the wheels' rims with clasped pins. The rods' other ends disappeared into a pair of horizontal cylinders with four tubes connecting to them, two to either cylinder.

Ernest was struck quiet by a strong feeling of déjà vu related to his studies. Was it an engine of some kind? He knew it wasn't a gasoline engine or any other modern engine. Thinking of engines, Ernest remembered some pictures he'd seen in his engineering history books. The realization was so sudden, so abrupt, he staggered. He was looking at a variety of extremely efficient steam-driven engine called a Stirling engine. The wheels turned from the force of a constantly pushing pressure governed by cool air and burning fuel. Since this was in a sealed system, it meant *any* heat, any fuel, could be used.

"Why are they powered by steam?" Ernest asked. "Electricity or gasoline would provide more power."

"As a former engineering student, you should know." Oru said. "Electric or gasoline engines wouldn't be powered by *any*thing, they'd be powered by *one* thing."

"What's the difference?"

Aural chuckled while Oru stroked her fur intensely, then she continued. "The Shifting Stones is the only place of this universe you have experienced. Aerth is our analogue of your Earth, similar to medieval Earth but with magic. *Real* magic."

"Of course," Oru took up the conversation now, "there are two kinds of magic. Fanciful and physical. One is based on imagination, the other is moved by faith. The point here is the practical nature of the thunclik. In medieval technology, electricity and gasoline are not practical because they aren't widely available. If Oruaural's thun-clik needed refueling stations throughout Aerth, that becomes more difficult if *any* mortals can see it."

Aural spoke up again. "Would your Earth's dark ages have worsened or improved, if the evil Machiavelli family had armored tanks? The natural development of society can only progress for the practical good if first they have the definition of morality by that which created it. If mortals set the foundation of morality for themselves, they can also redefine it until it suits their desires—good intentions or not. Remember that phrase among your people: 'The road to Hell is paved with good intentions.' This was what concerned your history's Leonardo Da Vinci; why he kept his designs from falling into the wrong hands. In times without electricity, an engine powered by heat itself means fuel is anything combustible. So thunclik aren't dependent on a narrow selection. Ah, look at that. Velosit is finished with Piv's torso."

Ernest turned to look at the muscular clerk. The idea that machines would even *have* muscles was strange, but this was a whole *world* of strange. On Earth, he had heard about shape-memory metals, like the alloy of nickel-titanium. These shape-memory metals behaved like regular organic muscles, or even took on new shapes altogether, when a voltage was applied. Velosit's thunclik muscles might've been something like that.

Instead of focusing on Velosit, Ernest stared at the thirty-something Caucasian woman behind him. He stared because Ernest knew the woman walking toward him only *looked* human. He also stared because she lacked an abdomen—her *thunclik* abdomen, anyway. The outfit she wore included a white blouse, gray ladies' business suit, and a matching skirt. Beneath this, her legs were surreal, because they looked like a normal pair of slender human legs with black stilettos. Attractive as her holographic femininity was, Ernest wondered how her torso was supported if the chassis wasn't there.

He pointed to Piv's arachnid chassis, still in the chamber. "I don't get it. Isn't that your engine?"

"Yes, it is." Piv nodded. "But only for when I need extra power. To test my repaired torso, I needed to move around before reattaching to my abdomen. Its energy storage was charged before reactivation of my crystalline brain and memory core. Now that we know my torso is fully functional..."

Piv transformed her appearance again. Since Ernest was looking this time when she changed, he saw her disguise fade, becoming the bronze body. Instead of the arachnid abdomen, she stood gracefully on three bronze pole-like legs. Rather than feet, she had pads made of a sturdy yet springy wire, with wheels underneath. He wasn't sure, but expected the wire could reshaped itself according to leave the "disguised" footprints. If she could lock her wheels, they'd probably be the same as human feet. But if they could *roll...* that's almost like they'd be little motorcycle tires.

Her change took less than half a minute, but he definitely needed more time just to see it. As they patiently waited for him, Ernest gathered his thoughts. Finally, he asked, "So... your thunclik have been visiting mortals in disguises like that? Why?"

Piv looked at Oruaural, both of whom nodded back to her.

"Mostly to prevent Bu' Zast and other evil Emissaries from interfering," Piv said. "They sometimes attempt to use the mortals' own mental disorders to manipulate them. Obviously, if we didn't disguise ourselves, many people would react with fear to our bronze metallic bodies. For Earth, resistance to evil is dependent on humanity's religious morals and free will, and of listening to your conscience. Our appearance can interfere with this, even if our intentions are good, so we protect Earth best in secret."

"Then why recruit me to tell a story about it?"

The Oruaurals wryly grinned. "Because they will see us as merely a fiction, a story. Some of humanity's greatest lessons in philosophy, and even science, have been allegorical—told through stories. *Hoom, hoom*, Velosit *is* fast! Piv's arachnid chassis is finished already."

Ernest looked at the now-empty chamber. "Where is it?"

"Her chassis has no sensors," Oru and Aural said, "but can be controlled remotely by Piv's torso. This is even easier if the area the chassis walks through is well known. *Many* thunclik have been through here *many* times. You might be boggled at how *many* 'manys' that means!"

Piv pointed down to the other end of the aisle and rolled toward it. As the chassis walked toward her, it seemed independent. Technically though, Piv *was* walking the chassis.

Ernest, Velosit, Oru, and Aural looked on as Piv reattached herself. The thunclik did this by extending her bronze legs until her torso was above the chassis, which lowered itself down to the floor. There was a hole where her torso inserted, and she lowered her legs inside. Then a series of clicking noises as Piv's two halves completed their connection.

While this finished, Ernest asked, "So what now?"

"The Now? Why, we're seeing it before us! Or is that in front? 'Before' may just as easily refer to the past, eh? *Eh?*"

Ernest groaned. "Perhaps I meant what *next*?"

"Right, you did!" The kooky pair threw back their heads and clapped. "Next, we all get to play hopscotch with space and time. You're going off to join Hahn and Laeljah. Even with Piv along, the thunclik of *that* time may not realize you're Oruaural's agent, even if Oruaural did give you a black suit and fancy shades! So..."

Aural beckoned Ernest closer. He leaned in. "Remember," She whispered, "the password is *not* 'swordfish.'"

"Okay," he whispered back. "So... what is it?"

"What's crazy and rhymes with 'tutu?'"

"What?"

"Not 'chicken-butt,' that's for sure!"

At the same time, Oru began twirling around her like a ballerina.

Ernest groaned, certain Oruaural was messing with him. Piv was almost done with her reboot. He decided that if he needed clearer answers, Piv would be the one to ask.

When Piv finished synchronizing herself, Oruaural both began to weep intensely. Even with their antics, Ernest felt strangely sad and bewildered.

"We are all ready to begin!" Oru and Aural both clapped loudly, and there was an overpowering light. It was not uncomfortable, but Ernest saw nothing else. Then there were sounds, *lots* of them. Of rushing wind. Of machine gears grinding. Of incredibly large objects moving nearby, moving *very* fast. Of a softened, resounding *crack* like distant thunder, but repeated steadily. Of electricity zapping and crackling.

Without completely realizing it, Ernest asked "Wha-what happened?" As he asked this, his vision slowly returned, and he saw the sounds. Or rather, saw what *made* them.

In front of him, Piv rested her spider chassis on the ground, while the quirky pair stood next to her. The Oruaurals wore such wide grins they almost seemed to split their heads in half. All three were quiet, but it was not quiet around them. Complex machines covered the walls with lights, wires, gears, tubing, valves, pumps, and some parts he had no name for. Above everything was an immensely thick band of coiling electricity, somehow confined into a ribbon that stretched from side to side with the subtlest of curves, as though forming a massive circle seen slightly edge-on. Through the mysteriously bound energy, something bent the light, or the air—perhaps space itself. Ernest wasn't sure, but thought it could have been any of these. As impressive as this was, behind the others was the source of the distant thunder, and it frightened him so much he felt like bolting away.

Objects moving so fast the resounding *cracks* were surely sonic booms, ripping the air and blasting them all by the passing wind. At first, he actually thought they were two massive trains, if trains floated in the air as they rocketed past each other. As above, so below, though the train below circled in the reverse direction of the one above.

Then he saw they weren't trains at all. They were *wheels,* spinning in opposite directions, moving so impossibly fast Ernest could only discern a vague, horizontal metallic form. The difference in directions at such impossible speed wouldn't allow him to focus on them without experiencing horrendous vertigo and a headache. As they moved, they became larger or smaller. This occurred in a steady rhythm, but he didn't recognize it. Instead he stared into the distant moon-sized void the wheels circled *around.*

Inside it was a swirling stream of gas and debris. Despite all that obscured it, in the center of the head-on swirl, was a circle of the darkest black he could imagine. Darker than even the earlier invaders' cloud portal. The black sphere was surrounded on its edge by a boundary of intense light that blurred into the darkness of the sphere. From its top and bottom streamed twin beams of energy that burned with such intensity they made Ernest rub his eyes in pain when he stared at the jets. It was *these* that Ernest recognized.

"You've harnessed the power of a *black hole?*"

Oru and Aural laughed. "Yes and no. It was *always* here. Oruaural wasn't. Though, Oruaural was aware of it from the black hole's beginning, and the rest of the Shifting Stones, for that matter. Oruaural will not explain; it'd take too long! No, you and Piv need to be going."

The wacky pair slowly raised their four-fingered hands up and curled their arms in an odd gesture. Ernest thought they were preparing to snap their fingers in unison. With an undefined feeling of great importance—ominous or auspicious, Ernest wasn't sure what to feel about it—they snapped their fingers. Nothing seemed to happen, which felt... anticlimactic.

He waited a moment. "What is *supposed* to be happening?"

The Oruaurals replied, "It still is. Just wait a minute. You'll be able to get on soon enough."

As they said this, Ernest realized the pair of immense wheels were slowing down. They were still impossible to completely focus on, but they *were* slowing. Enough that he saw the wheels resolving into hoops of braided bronze cables with pod-like shapes. Singularly, each cable was thicker than many trees he had seen. Together, they were thicker than any semi-truck trailer. Bulging out from the cables, the pods were marked by windows in their domes.

It boggled his mind to think it could move so fast its passing alone seemed to try tearing everything apart. Now, it slowed down as if it was a mere merry-go-round. For all the details he didn't understand Ernest resolved his trust to faith, because the hope of success was than thinking of failure. If there were unknowns, perhaps an explanation would help, or *not*, or add more confusion *with* the explanation. If God had a plan even for this, he'd survive. If he was merely crazy now, at least it wasn't boring.

For all the incomprehensibly fast speed, perhaps *many* times the speed of sound, now a pod was slowing to a stop facing them. Such power demonstrated merely by the Oruaurals' command. It amazed Ernest, which was perhaps why he realized at the moment, Velosit wasn't there.

"Why isn't Velosit with us?"

The others looked at him as if he'd declared he was going to eat all his clothes, slather his naked body in butter, then lick the whole floor.

"Because Velosit is in the *assembly* offices," Piv said. "He's fast, but his behavioral skillset is optimized towards organization, parts inventory or recall, and strategic design of thunclik bodily forms. His talent is in the assembly offices, but *not* for battle. Now, Oruaural will help us get into the Observational Relativistic Chrono Centrifuge, and instruct you for—"

"The ORCC!" Oru and Aural interjected. "You will need to get inside the ORCC!"

"Yes," Piv sighed. "My Emissary prefers referring to it that way... but never explained why. Apparently, it is—"

It was then that Ernest got the joke. He laughed aloud, and Piv waited, irritated. After his laughing abated, she continued in annoyance. "*Apparently*, it is a source of great amusement for Oruaural, instead of the self-explanatory name. Can you clarify this? Oruaural told me I will be the only thunclik ever to understand."

"Yes!" the Oruaurals said happily. "Go on and tell her. But *whisper* it."

Ernest blushed, then leaned toward Piv. After he explained, she also laughed for a few moments.

"Yes," Aural said with a grin. "Now that you're all done with that..." Aural stretched her wings as if considering flying into the void occupied by a *black hole*, which felt entirely plausible given what Oru and Aural were.

Oru continued the description, "You need to understand how to use the ORCC. It may seem as though only an on/off switch is needed for this, but it is more than that."

Then Oru turned toward Piv. "Open the pod bay doors, Piv."

There was a hint of laughter, but Ernest wasn't sure if this was a deliberate reference to *2001: A Space Odyssey*. It could have been, as Oruaural was an insane, reality-altering, interdimensional, cosmically powerful entity who was *uncannily* familiar with Earth's pop culture.

Piv walked up to a small button console near the edge of the massive void. Whatever she typed in the panel caused the two dome-shaped pods facing them to open and two rows of steps to unfold from the pods' sides, much like that of many mid-size airplanes.

A catwalk extended to the pod above. Aural and Piv went up, as Oru led Ernest to the one below.

"Now," the Emissary of Madness was saying, "remember that because Piv's personality core wasn't backed up at your exiting time, if she gets destroyed again, it's permanent. Really dead. No reconstruction with Velosit or anyone. But that's not what you need to focus on right now."

Ernest was so bothered by this revelation that he stared in shock at the thunclik above him.

"*Dead?*" He gazed at Oru. "Wh-what do you mean? Why?"

Oru glared at him. "I... just... *told*... you. Even if you need to ignore it for now, it's a warning you and Piv will *need*. You're not only going through time; you'll be leaving the Shifting Stones. You're going to the *real* world, with *real* risks! Some people there, especially in the Grefarn Empire, think we're fictional characters. Piv will have *no* backups, so you need to know the risk, yet face it! Remember this important warning for your After, but focus on the *Now*. The most important thing is to know how to control your pod. As to that—"

Oru gestured to the drop-down stairs and gently prodded Ernest inside.

"—the pod's magic is controlled by focusing your awareness of it and your intentions. This—"

"Me? Magic? But I can't—"

"No," Oru interrupted. "Don't interrupt, and do not doubt! You're from Earth, which means you don't have any natural awareness of using magic, but any creature with a complex neural system can use magic. Using it *intelligently* is something else. Fortunately, Earth has always been aware of magic as a concept, though only recently started to use it practically."

"*What?*"

Ernest stared at Oru, then at the pod's interior. There was a padded chair with a strange texture that had... well, he didn't know. It was a peculiar contradiction, of both rough and smooth. Whatever it was, he suspected it was not Corinthian leather. Facing the chair was a large, crystalline, desk-sized prism covered with mostly parallel angular lines. Some lines intersected. Standing upright above the strange crystal desk, two crystalline rods shone with refracted light.

Oru spoke up. "Oruaural knows this is difficult to understand, let alone even *activate*, so Oruaural will do that for you."

He pointed to it and shouted, "ORCC, I choose you!"

Immediately the crystal desk lit up with holographic projections of transparent, colorful light. Framed by the crystalline rods, it now served as a viewscreen display. There were also subdued, barely noticeable sounds... like notifications?

Oru indicated the display, the middle of which bore the image of a holographic sphere inside a thick holographic line. At the top, was an identical sphere inside an identical line.

"This is something you must *not* lose track of," Oru pointed to the display. "It contains the direct awareness of *all* your projected subatomic spins, velocities, electromagnetic charges, energy states, and masses. All the defining data of the pod and yourself, collected in a single expression. The sphere in the center of the first display represents this pod and everything in it. The line—"

"Uh..." Ernest interrupted nervously. "I know you said I shouldn't interrupt, but I must ask this to understand. You refer to this as magic, and say I'm able to use it. But this isn't magic, it's science and applied physics. Why do you call it magic?"

Oru peered curiously at him. "Because that's exactly what it is! Does your science completely understand quantum physics or the entirety of energy? If you focus your magic to heat something up, its atoms will spin faster, while others must slow down. For every fire, so too, must the cold be as dire. Isn't that what magic is in fantasy?"

Ernest waved dismissively to the holograms "Well, I've never heard of any magic like this. *Why* shouldn't I lose track?"

Oru curled his tongue into a nostril. "Because the slightest distraction may doom us all. *Doom!* **Doom!** It may *doom* us ALL! *Doom...* Anyway, the line is a projection of this pod's motion through time and space. Piv's pod is here."

He pointed to the sphere above in the second display. "You must never lose track of hers either. If you do, the uncertainty principle may send you and Piv off course, directly crashing to spin into the black hole, ripping apart, or vaporizing into subatomic plasma. Any of these may happen if you lose your awareness, so you *must* keep your focus on the spheres, and concentrate on staying inside the lines. Moving through time is the relativity of observing yourself and Piv moving in opposite directions. If you're moving at half the speed of light, while observing Piv coming at you with the same speed, then the combined effect of both *is* the speed of light. Piv's timeframe will also drag backward as she observes you the same way. Any questions?"

Difficult though it was, Ernest had kept quiet through the rest. The whole idea of physics as "magic" was not what he expected. Especially in the relativistic physics of time travel.

Oru's seriousness made him want to ask why he shouldn't doubt. If doubt drove the expectation that something special would *not* happen, then perhaps faith was the expectation that something special *would*. In many religious stories, the miracles seemed to highlight belief. In all the stories he'd ever heard about learning to use magic, there'd been something about practicing. But Oru seemed to imply magic was an awareness of physics *and* belief.

Ernest thought about that ring... the Eye of the Beholder. It was "effected," wasn't it? Were magic and physics the same? Was it really as simple as imagining something, concentrating, and *believing* with faith?

"Yes!" Oru interrupted Ernest's thoughts. "That's it exactly! Well... also determined by the source and if it doesn't conflict with that source. The source of the magic determines the ultimate nature of how that power is used. For this reason, some sources are generally considered forbidden under *any* circumstances. In some ways, it's the most important thing to consider. Ekallr's power will never act against Ekallr. Now that you know all you need, Oruaural will be going now. Farewell, or as Hahn would say, leaving can be a greeting later!"

Stunned, Ernest paused for almost a minute as Oru backed out of the pod. Just as the Emissary was stepping off the stairs, Ernest rushed for the hatch.

"W-wait!" he pleaded. "What am I supposed to do? You can't just leave without telling me more about the controls and how to use them!"

Oru shook his head. "No more of that from Oruaural, because Oruaural has already *told* you how to operate it, and you thought correctly. Oruaural is not going to waste the rest of quadrant three repeating things, and our author needs to move things along. Besides, Oruaural *knows* you're going to survive this! Uh... somehow. Oruaural apologizes in advance for the concussion, but that happens in places that aren't well-maintained." The folding stairs lifted as Ernest frantically asked about a *concussion*, but Oru ignored him. "You know all you need to know. Bye!"

Oru gave a friendly wave goodbye, then the hatch closed completely.

As the whole pod lurched under his feet, Ernest flinched. Still concerned he didn't understand enough and unwilling to trust the strange chair, he tried the displays. His ring didn't seem to respond either, so he was stuck.

Although he hadn't tried to start it, Ernest realized the pod was moving on its own. If the activation was automated, why did he need to keep track of the pods? Another strong heave and he almost staggered. Lunging for the chair, he realized his first impression of the chair *not* being leather was correct.

When he dropped into it, he immediately felt a strange adhesiveness from it, rendering him completely paralyzed from the neck down. Then he noticed its surface *moving*, like a giant chair-shaped amoeba, stretching itself over his body to absorb and digest him.

Panicking, he yelled, "Oruaural? Piv? This damn chair's *eating* me!"

"No, it isn't," Piv's disembodied voice explained. "It's a momentum negation chair. It neutralizes your body's G-forces so you don't smear against the wall. Stop worrying, access your controls, focus on the pods, and concentrate on staying in those lines! We must minimize communication."

Following the reminders, Ernest looked to the screen. When he did, it streaked close to his head, stopping abruptly about a hands-length away. So much he recoiled. A holographic keyboard was in easy access to his hands, sending light circling around his fingertips.

Even in the mysterious chair, everything shook like an earthquake. Focusing on calming down, he searched his memory for what he had been told about the controls. Imagine, concentrate, and believe. To keep his attention on the pod in the screen and imagine the sphere. The pod's rough jostling continued, but... lessened? Encouraged, he concentrated more on the display's sphere. It was bouncing harshly in the calculated route and constantly accelerating. But now he pictured the pod in his mind, focusing on it staying inside the line. The pod calmed down even more, increasing his confidence.

As it all began to settle, Ernest glanced at what looked like a speedometer. When he realized what the number was, he gasped. If it was accurate, his speed was over 16,777,000 miles per hour! He didn't have the exact speed, because the last three digits were increasing so fast they blurred. Next to the mph label was an accelerating percentage of lightspeed. He couldn't even *begin* to comprehend how fast that was, other than *extremely fast* and getting *faster*. Surely the pod moved many times the speed of sound, but there were no sonic booms. None that he noticed, anyway. Either he was moving so fast that his own sonic booms couldn't keep up with him, or something was suppressing the noise. He might actually catch up with his own previous sonic booms at this speed.

If he was traveling faster than the speed of light—Ernest knew at least this much about relativistic effects—he shouldn't be able to see anything in front. Did Oruaural use their power to allow this inside the pod? Remembering Oruaural prompted Ernest to look at Piv's pod in the display. As he did so, he noticed the subtlest of light blue changing from its former white. He'd heard about redshift, but this was blue. If so, this meant he was approaching the speed of light. In the display, the image of Piv's pod grew fainter and flickered. He didn't know why, but he was sure it was important.

The speed was now greater than 173,257,000 miles per hour. If he wasn't already moving at lightspeed, he might well reach it before he knew it. Human science still didn't know exactly what happened at that speed... Ernest squinted at the armrest. Somehow its edges had a strange, strong fuzziness, tinted blue. As he began to think about this, the pod bumped and vibrated. Quickly, Ernest turned back to the display, focusing on settling the pod down.

The edges of everything blurred more and more. He allowed himself only a vague awareness of this. It didn't make sense. While he couldn't focus on it, the edges of everything were blurred with deep blue.

If he could have looked around, Ernest would have seen that while everything in front of him was a deep, cobalt blue, everything behind him was a solid brick red. The pod's desk, floor, and windshield exhibited a strange visual effect. Dots of intense blue light were scattered about, moving in straight lines or spiraling circles. It was almost distracting enough to be dangerous. He risked a quick glance up at Piv's pod above. Instead, there was only a dark purplish-blue ring as wide as a city road.

In the distance, everything was also blue, but a much lighter shade. The area directly ahead was the *darkest* of the blue, almost a deep purple. Piv's pod was a massive, ring-shaped tube with a texture reminiscent of cotton, so dark purple it was almost black. It flickered, just like in the display. Ernest realized while his own sphere wasn't flickering, the speed now read over 335,200,000 miles per hour. Piv's flickering was a strobe light. It felt so surreal. He didn't know exactly how fast he was moving, but knew it was a sizable fraction of the speed of light. The velocity's digits changed faster than he could read them, and the last few were blank. Sort of. Replacing them was a series of vague oval-ish forms in the display, with the size and spacing apparently matching the numbers.

The numbers were changing so fast they became mere ovals of light now. Piv's pod flickered so *much* Ernest felt the strobe would cause a seizure. Suddenly the display's sphere intensified brightly, then abruptly vanished. Outside the windshield, the same thing happened to Piv's motion-blurred pod. The light flash was so distracting that for a brief instant, his own pod started to shake and lurch again. He concentrated to settle down his pod again. Staring in the display, Piv's pod was... moving backward? Puzzled, he looked out the windshield.

Outside, the blue was darker. Not only was Piv's pod moving backward, it was also a strong crimson *red*. Confused why, but avoiding distraction, he looked to the display and noticed a *new* number. Labeled "countdown to selected time, automated egress setting." The number showed ninety-eight percent remaining.

Then ninety-seven percent, then ninety-six percent.

The percentage dropped a single digit every ten seconds. While he waited, the strange dots of light and blurred edges became more intense. Ernest determined that as soon as possible, he needed to ask Oruaural about this and demand an explanation for everything. Especially why this whole insane contraption treated relativistic physics as if it was a tremendous carnival ride.

Seventy-one percent, Seventy percent, Sixty-nine percent.

As the remaining time counted down, Ernest wondered what this was all for. The implication was of being sent somewhere to meet a "Hahn" and "Laeljah," whoever they were. But this machine wasn't "sending" him anyplace if it was a giant, super-fast hula hoop. Nor had he been told why that pair were so vitally important to Oruaural's intentions. Apparently, his purpose here was to tell their story. He wanted to figure that out, but couldn't concentrate here.

The "automated egress" was forty-two percent finished. Forty-one percent, forty percent, thirty-nine percent.

The dots of light outside the windshield were flickering streaks now. The purplish-blue shift was lighter. The hoop of Piv's pod was a lighter red, almost pink. If their pods were moving beyond lightspeed, then he shouldn't be able to even see Piv's hoop, let alone anything at all. He'd be traveling too fast for any light to reach his eyes. The sight of Piv's pod should have shifted in the electro-magnetic-spectrum beyond what any perception. Maybe this was some other strange "magic" of physics?

Ernest checked the "automated egress," and saw it read seven percent.

Six percent, five percent, four percent, three percent.

Abruptly, the light outside the windshield was dingier. Two percent. Sooty. Like some grittiness floating in the air tinted the purple with a hint of gray. Piv's pod had the barest hint of red, as if it was copper, not bronze.

One percent. A flashing zero percent, then Ernest felt a slight pull forward, like when you're cruising to a red stoplight. But commutes never had a white flash or strong blueshift. Ernest realized the pod was slowing down the same way as before. He looked forward to getting more details from Oruaural. Ernest expected to be irritated, but he was thrown into this with the distinct instruction that if he didn't figure it out, he'd be *destroyed*.

Eventually, the blueshift disappeared. They were still moving, but the velocity was over 18,000,000 miles per hour and dropping fast. The view outside appeared again, and something looked different. When the speed dropped below 144,000 miles per hour, he noticed the black hole's debris field was much smaller. Almost non-existent.

Soon, the motion-blurred hoop of Piv's pod lost all trace of the blueshift. The speed was 64,780 miles per hour and still dropping. It seemed strange to Ernest the chair would be able to handle G-forces, especially light-speed, but he also had no idea how it worked. Maybe that was why motion sickness wasn't a problem—not that he complained. As he watched, the speed finally slowed enough that he could see things clearly outside.

Although the pod was still moving, he could see the walls looked far different now. They appeared completely forsaken, with perhaps centuries of ruin and corrosion. Even for this place, it was a drastic change. But for what-ever reason everything else looked older, Piv's pod may have been new.

The pods continued slowing gently. When they did at last stop, the chair moved its amoeba-like substance, but off instead of *over* him. The instant it let him go, he jumped up quickly, crossing his fingers in the clichéd vampire warding from movies.

"Piv?" No response. He frowned and tried again. "Piv? Oru? Uh... Aural?"

All was quiet, so he looked around. Ernest grabbed the door's manual release and opened it to a hiss of air pressure. As he stared at the deterioration, he coughed a bit from the dusty, stale, somewhat stinky air. No one was there.

"*Piv*?!" He yelled up to her pod, concerned. More silence, so he ran up the stairs to Piv's pod. As he got there, he heard another pressurized hiss and the pod opened.

"Do not worry!" she called. "I am unharmed."

Ernest sighed with relief. He didn't know how he'd handle this by himself, and needed a friend, especially here.

As she stepped out of her pod, the metal staircase groaned ominously. Piv stopped and withdrew. Gesturing down, she said, "Go back down. The platform may collapse under our combined weight. Don't worry about me. I'll get there just fine."

Studying the rusty stairs, he conceded she was probably right, but still worried. Wasn't her metallic body much heavier? Although moving carefully, each new groan of the stairs made him wince. After getting off, he looked back, equal parts curious and concerned. Piv emerged again, then looked toward the bottom landing at a pipe bolted firmly to the wall.

Then casually... *suddenly*, a cable shot from her chest. With a loud *thunk*, the cable with a heavy metal cylinder, whirled tightly around the metal pipe. Then the cable quickly spooled back into Piv's chest, drawing her rapidly forward, looking *more* like a spider than ever.

She leaped from the pod and dropped down below the platform. Ernest rushed to the edge and looked down, just in time for her to leap up. Startled, he jumped back in shock as Piv landed heavily on the floor.

"Hey!"

"What?" Piv retorted. "I told you I'd be fine. So, you ready to go out?"

Ernest stared, then shook his head vigorously. "No. I need to know what the hell happened. I need to go ask Oru or Aural what this whole demented oversized bicycle wheel thing was for. I'm not going to do anything else until I get some answers from Oru or Aural!"

"We can't do that!" she insisted. "We need to go off and find Hahn and Laeljah first."

"No," he insisted right back, "I'm supposed to record some story. How can I do that if I don't understand these things?"

Piv held up her hand. "You will understand as we continue our narrative. Besides, you don't need to understand *everything* to do *something*. That's why we're going out to join Hahn and Laeljah."

"That's just repeating things!" Ernest complained. "I told you, I won't do anything until Oruaural explains more! If I don't understand this crazy place, then how do I know I won't die? Where's Oru or Aural?"

This time, Piv was the one staring. "That's exactly what this is all about. Oruaural isn't here. So, we need to look *for* Oruaural! See? You got it already."

Ernest grumbled angrily, "That doesn't make *any* sense! Why can't—"

Without warning, a pipe fell on his head, knocking him out.

Frustrated, Piv sighed vaporously from her mouth. Then she tugged the unconscious Ernest to a golden pad inset with the wall. Under the safety of its alcove, she checked his heartbeat and other vitals. With her crystalline eyes, sensors, and data analysis, Piv diagnosed a major concussion. Since they were alone, remaining calm was important.

Reaching down to her hip, Piv opened a metal cover in her metallic skin. Then she grabbed inside a power and data transfer cable. As she pulled it out, Piv felt the wall with her other hand. When she found the marker she was looking for, she pushed the wall's hidden panel in and up, revealing a data port. After inserting the cable, she held Ernest to her body while sending teleportation coordinates and a large power pulse into the gold pad's controls.

Knowing ahead of time the pad would have a delayed response after pulsing the cable, she pulled it back into herself. The access hatch closed and twenty seconds later, the pad glowed. After the teleportation, all that remained, was a little blood on the floor.

QUADRANT FOUR:

FINDING DIRECTION IN TIME

When Ekallr tests us, **he** does not need proof of what he already knows; that proof is for *us* to buoy our faith. If difficulty vanquishes mortal effort, pride may fail and seem like certain death. Faith in Ekallr helps us face even lesser threats, for that courage comes from *beyond* the mortal.

– Archpriest of the Whistling
Steppes Monastery

After the bizarre experience of the ORCC, Ernest tried to recall why he was standing in a church. Did the crazy machine send him there? Was it Oruaural? Formal decorations were placed throughout the church, and a large crowd filled its pews. Ernest wasn't sure what was going on.

There was three tuxedo-clad **m**en on the left side of the altar, and on the right, women in satin dresses. Pastor Ericson wore his ceremonial vestments. The same church he attended for Sunday. To add to his confusion, Ernest saw... himself in the third person. The other Ernest wore a silver suit, facing the crowd seated in the pews.

A wedding.

Again, Ernest wondered how or why he was here. Even if the blackhole-powered whirling insanity and the rest were symptoms of madness, wouldn't he have some memory of walking into the church? Of the breakfast he ate? He wondered which one was the dream and who he was marrying.

As if in answer, the organ's twenty-feet tall bronze pipes resonated with the "Wedding March" and the doors opened. A veiled woman in a white gown with a conical bell of lightweight silk stepped into the church. In her dark hair was a garland of grape leaves. Despite the veil, he knew who this was, walking resolutely to him on her father's arm. If she had ignored her fear of marriage, this would have been the future for Ernest and Jeannette. But she *had* listened to her anxiety, so Ernest was confused why he saw this.

Pastor Ericson went through the pledges then for some strange reason, emphasized the next part loudly. "If there are any *objections* as to why these two should *not* be wed, let them speak *now* or forever hold their peace."

What Ernest saw next was difficult to understand. Although Jeannette didn't step away or stop the ceremony, some alternate version of her tried to. As if in nightmarish mitosis, a *new* version of Jeannette "divided" and pushed out of her body. No one reacted in any way. The second Jeannette was as invisible to the crowd as the observing Ernest. This alternate Jeannette screamed at herself, to no avail. As her young son Joshua proudly stepped forward, he held up a small pillow, smiled joyfully at his mother, and presented the rings. Angry Jeannette lunged at him, still screaming, but again, there was no reaction.

The other Ernest beamed at Jeannette and her son, pushing the ring onto her finger. "With this ring, I do pledge my life and my heart."

The alternate Jeannette tried to slap it away, but the first Jeannette took the other ring and pushed it onto Ernest's finger. "With this ring, I do pledge my life and my heart."

"By the authority of God," Pastor Ericson said, "in the sight of these witnesses, I declare that this man and woman are husband and wife. You may kiss the bride."

Ernest watched himself and Jeannette smile. It was the most contented thing he ever saw. They kissed, even as the alternate Jeannette screeched and threw herself at them. But instead of knocking the newlyweds to the floor, she passed through like a ghost.

"Damn you!" she screamed. "You saw your parents end their happiness in that evil divorce! You *know* what happened! This will never be more than a fairy tale! *Stop* this!"

Jeannette turned and recognized the observing Ernest. He tensed in fear as she bolted to him.

"Baby, baby, baby," she pleaded, "you *know* I love you, but you remember what I've said, how this is all just a silly daydream. Remember how this is doomed to fail in a horrible divorce? Please stop it! We can still love each other. We don't *need* to ever marry to love. We..." She started crying loudly.

Confused and concerned, Ernest spoke. "But you realize... uh... that's what marriage is meant for, right?

It's a public declaration. Even when strangers see only the rings, they know we love each other. Why wouldn't we push ourselves to the highest expression of our feelings for each other? It's a declaration of our loyalty. Others may forget theirs, but you're saying we'd fail before we ever gave it a chance. If you give up on something before you attempt it, what if you're missing out on the deepest happiness you'd ever know?"

"My parents' lives were turned upside down!" Her face contorted in violent rage. "They would never have experienced that pain if they didn't marry! Your parents' marriage is a fluke, a freak against their inner natures! Marriage comes with rules, obligations, with the expectation I *must* confine myself. I won't let anyone see where they can hurt me!"

"But my parents are proud of their love," Ernest tried again. "That's not behaving foolishly. You see your son doing something awesome, and you feel proud, don't you? Doesn't that make you a better mother? He feels happier from your approval as a parent. If you can't approve of my excitement to love you as your husband, it's like you're ashamed of me. Please, why can't you accept my love, my pride for you, and share our lives together?"

Angry Jeannette stared at Ernest quietly for a moment, then screamed. "All I wanted was the make-believe! The safe! But you wanted *more*, you wanted the impossible—a happy marriage! I don't care if it's fake, I want my make-believe!"

"That's utterly incomprehensible," Ernest countered. "A gold bar is valuable for people wanting the real thing.

Is make-believe money ever going to buy you anything? Plenty of couples are happy together because they don't sacrifice their love for little things. They—"

She glared at him *murderously* now, all while the other Ernest and Jeannette, now happily married, walked to their families in smiling celebration. Suddenly, angry Jeannette lunged at his first-person self, tearing the body apart.

Bolting from the bed in terror, Ernest's body covered in sweat. As he gasped, he looked around. At first, what Ernest saw confused him because his mind was still clouded from sleep and the nightmare. Upon recalling his memory, he concentrated a little more. Though he didn't know how he got there, he was still alive. The bed was a big king size and slightly... bowl-shaped, like a large, circular satellite dish made into a mattress. His head throbbed painfully, but when Ernest tried sitting up, the throbbing worsened.

There was a sound, a crunching noise. But chewing. Chewing something crunchy. It didn't sound like a wet crunchiness, like celery. It was more a dry crunchiness, like granola, but with a sudden, cracking crunch. Was someone chewing a hard candy bar? Here? He supposed it was possible.

Ernest sat up again, ignoring the pain and blinking his eyes. The room reminded him of a hospital, colored in a pastel seafoam green. There was a small table on one side and a couple of windows. On his left, the window showed a spectacular view of the planetoid city Delirium from an orbital altitude. Floating asteroids surrounded him. Ernest wondered if he was *on* one of those islands floating in Delirium's sky.

The other window was directly across from him. Through it, he saw a thunclik, but it wasn't Piv. Ernest waved to get her attention. She stopped chewing on the crunchy something-or-other and entered the room.

"Good to see you're awake. First, my name is Calia Syne. Second, you are in one of the Bone Rooms of the Shifting Stones—a hospital. Third, you had a major concussion, but your head is healing nicely. Does this answer your most important questions?"

Ernest blinked and nodded.

"Good," Calia said. "I'm sure you have more to talk about, but I have questions, too. Do you feel comfortable cooperating?"

Ernest looked at her. "Cooperate? Why do I need to? What if I don't?"

"No harm will come to you, but we won't help you or the thunclik you arrived with. Neither of you will be detained, but neither of you will receive any help from us. I presume you require clarification of cooperation? We merely wish you to explain why you are both here."

"Why we are here?" he echoed.

"Yes," Calia said. "We have never encountered your specific species before, and nor is there any record of Piv. Although we have no assurance of your intentions, we must verify that neither of you is hostile. We admit you may be allied with the Stones. Although she is a mystery to us, Piv *is* a thunclik."

Ernest thought about this. "This conversation feels guarded. Why are you so concerned about my intentions?"

Calia's eyes flashed like Piv's oddly familiar manner. "Because the Shifting Stones are at war."

"War?" Ernest frowned. "What are you talking about? They never mentioned anything about a war. Well, I suppose there was that battle... but after, Oruaural never said any—"

"*Oruaural*?! You've *talked* with Oruaural?"

Taken aback, Ernest stared. "Ye-es... uh, isn't that—"

Calia gave a halting gesture. "No... before we go further, I must be sure of something. What is the password?"

"Password? What do you mean, password?"

"If you spoke with Oruaural before arriving here, weren't you given a password?"

Ernest closed his eyes and searched his memory. Shaking his head, he replied, "No, I wasn't given a password, just told what it *isn't*. Like, not 'chicken-butt.' I was very annoyed. I mean, how am I supposed to remember a word I'm not told? Where's Oruaural? I want to yell at—"

Partly through Ernest's recollection, Calia tensed suddenly in surprise. As if raising herself on her spider legs increased her alertness by way of her posture.

"I must tell you now, Oruaural's not here."

"Then where—"

Calia took a deep breath. "Oruaural doesn't exist."

Ernest scowled. "Come on, stop messing with me. Where's Oruaural?"

"I told you, Oruaural doesn't exist—not physically anyway. Please do *not* leave your bed. I must discuss this privately with the other thunclik."

She turned her arachnid body toward the door and left.

When Calia returned, Piv stood behind her. Ernest had thought of some new questions while he waited. Questions about Oruaural's nonexistence, which didn't make sense, even if it related to that insane carnival ride. He didn't understand a lot about relativistic physics, but at lightspeed, time should have slowed down to an almost glacial pace. Not that he'd have noticed, but the difference in his time rate versus the rest of the universe's would mean... he was flung *forward* in time. Maybe even thousands of years. Enough time for a lot of things to happen—even for an Emissary to die? If Oruaural no longer existed, how would he get back to Earth?

"Piv, that crazy hula hoop thing sent us through time, right?"

"Yes," she agreed. "That's quite perceptive of you."

"'Hula hoop thing?'" Calia repeated as a question.

"Yes," Piv explained, "it's involved with the Prognostication of Oruaural's Transmogrification."

The other thunclik's eyes widened in surprise and recognition. Clearly, this was important, though Ernest didn't know why. For all the questions he had, this discussion brought up an issue that alarmed him in a brand new way.

"Piv," he said, "how will I get back to Earth if—"

"If Oruaural **d**oesn't exist yet?" Piv finished. "Because to get back home, you'll need to help Oruaural materialize."

Ernest puzzled over this, but expected he wouldn't get any more information. He turned to the medical thunc**lik**. "Calia, if you haven't encountered my... ah, species, how is it you are able to speak with me? Surely, your language is not English."

The thunclik smiled.

"That is *also* perceptive of you," Calia said. "Yes, English is not my natural language. I speak it because Piv transferred her st**o**red data of the English language and use of it to me. It was only language data transfer, nothing else. During my discussion with her, Piv answered all of my remaining questions. You have indeed talked with Oruaural. We must assist you on your way to fulfill Oruaural's wishes. Is there anything else you intend to ask?"

Ernest blinked again. This was a very sudden turn of attitude. Even though he hadn't told them much about himself, it seemed as though they completely trusted him now. First, the neutral attitude of questions only, now it was full support. It was so sudden he almost didn't realize its significance.

"W-why were you so concerned about security earlier?"

"Because it is part of why we have reason to be concerned," Piv said. "As was mentioned, the Shifting Stones is under a condition of war. We need to be sure our enemies aren't infiltrating this plain, because they have used *many* tricks. Now that Calia knows what could not be faked, she understands you and I were sent on behalf of Oruaural."

Though unclear, it didn't feel like a runaround to him.

"Okay," Ernest said while trying to remember. "Where are these two people Oruaural wanted us to find? Uh… Hahn and Laeljah? How would they help us?"

Piv's smile broadened. "Moving along—good! They are in the world of the mortals. Aerth."

"Aerth?"

"Yes, Aerth." Piv paused for a moment. "You know we are in a different universe than your Earth's universe. You are familiar with Earth's religious concepts of Heaven and Hell—distinctly different places for distinctly different natures, and the natures of choices that led to either. Earth is a place for mortals to freely choose what decisions to make. In that sense, Heaven is for encouraging the virtuous, as the reward for pursuing that nature. The Shifting Stones is for those who have lost the ability to rationally choose, not knowing what the difference is, or those who are ruled by disorder. Hell, meant to confine those who were warned against evil, is eternal punishment. As Earth is to humans for choosing their fates, so Aerth is to mortals in this universe. A planet, a world, for souls to freely understand themselves."

Ernest looked at the two thunclik thoughtfully. "Okay, but… that still doesn't explain to me why I was sent into the future or why Oruaural doesn't exist."

Calia and Piv shared an odd look, then Piv explained. "That's because Oruaural doesn't exist *yet*. We weren't sent into the future; we were sent into the past. I'd explain if

I could, but we have little time. As I've said, you'll understand better when we experience it."

Ernest frowned. "The *past*? Why didn't you say anything?"

"I'm saying something *now*," Piv deadpanned. "I was sure you already knew. Oruaural alluded to it several times during those discussions. Besides, what does it matter? You're here in the Shifting Stones' past, anyway. Our audience will find a lengthy explanation boring."

Calia held up a hand and looked around. "Audience? There seemed to be mention of this in the data transfer, but... nobody else is here."

Piv paused for a moment. "Open your data transfer port."

Calia nodded. Ernest gasped to see Piv feed the cable to the other. Both the thuncliks' eyes flashed just like... internet router lights! If they were transferring data, internet routers made sense. But *what* internet? While thinking about internet routers, Ernest saw Calia's eyes widen again in surprise.

"He's writing about us even as we're talking?"

"Yes," Piv told her.

"What? Who's writing about what?" Ernest blurted.

"Hush!" Piv admonished, then said to Calia, "He's going to describe our trip on the stormfish next."

Ernest pursed his lips, wondering what this was about now. He didn't have long to wait. Their eyes stopped flashing, and Piv pulled her data cable out.

Calia gasped excitedly. "There is a solution? The Shifting Stones will not—"

A loud **boom** shook the entire room with the sounds of screaming metal. The air filled with what sounded like a World War II air raid siren.

"What the hell is going on?!" Ernest screamed.

Calia looked at him with a strange expression of hope. "Another invasion attempt. But this time it must be because they know you're here! All we haVe time to say is they're trying to stop you as the prophecy's herald."

A distant boom thundered elsewhere.

"What... why?" Ernest yelled. "How can we help?!"

Calia looked back at him as another blast filled the air. The floor started breaking into branching cracks, then tilted down. The room didn't collapse underneath yet, but it did stagger them.

Calia shouted, "You need to leave! Piv, get him to the stormfish!"

Piv nodded and tugged Ernest's arm. As they dashed into the hallway, it was filled by various thunclik and other personnel. They all responded to the attack by running to artillery positions and other duties. Another crashing sound, as dust fell from the ceiling.

"What do we need to do?" Ernest panted.

"We need to leave," Piv said. "Follow me to the transport as quickly as possible."

He found her calmness in the turmoil strange. "Leave? But we need to fight back!"

Another explosion and a wall fell. Outside, Ernest saw several monsters crawling like tanks, big as dinosaurs. They smashed their way through the courtyard of the hospital. Strapped on their backs were heavy javelin throwers. They launched barbed metal bolts the size of telephone poles at the hospital. Four were already stuck in the outside walls and the ground. One of the hospital's artillery weapons was on fire, partly collapsed. A bolt on one of the monsters finished cranking back, then shot with all the force of a guided missile.

When it struck the wall only fifteen feet away, the impact's branching cracks were nearly forty feet long. Ernest fell as the floor dropped below, but Piv shot her grapple just in time to catch him.

"Can you teleport up here?" she called down.

Ernest gripped the cable, dangling like a fish on a hook. He stared up at Piv, then realized what she asked. As he concentrated on teleporting, his stomach felt somewhat nauseous, and slightly dizzy. There was sort of a sensation of the platform above him, then...

Abruptly his awareness snapped back to himself. "I-I don't think I can! Can you bring me up?"

Piv nodded and started pulling. After clasping his hand, she gave him a full-face breathing mask.

"What's this—" he started.

In response she strapped it on. "We don't have a lot of time. The sleeper cell will try stopping us by any method possible, from getting out of the Stones. If you see smoke, control your fear as much you can. Giving in to it will help the smoke overwhelm you, even *with* the mask!"

"Sleeper cell? Smoke?" Ernest asked. "What are you talking about? Smoke is just smoke. Maybe it would obscure things, but—"

There was the sound of someone yelling in another hallway and something like a grenade.

"Yukar! Bu' Zast za *yukar* tuesh-fo urool!" The voice contained raw, undisguised *hatred*.

The other hallway's doors burst open, and a berserking Vungir charged. He threw something at Piv and Ernest, which belched forth a constant stream of smoke so black it might've been pure carbon soot. Yelling herself, Piv tackled the Vungir. Even so, smoke rapidly filled the corridor, blocking everything. Ernest felt a sudden combination of unexplained fear and extreme sadness. The breakup's depression, the fears in his nightmares. Ernest felt himself filled with a compulsion to *run*, to flee the smothering darkness.

As he tried to retreat, Ernest felt a hand clamp on his shoulder. Certain it was some evil demon trying to eat his soul, he tried to throw the monster off but heard Piv.

"No!" she cried out. "That's *my* hand! Control your fear. The smoke reacts to your feelings!"

"P-p-piv?" He still wanted to bolt. "W-why is e-everything trying to kill me?"

"Do not fear, it is I. I know you're nearly overwhelmed by fear, but you *must* calm yourself. I tied up that terrorist. Nothing will hurt you if you keep *calm*."

Ernest sobbed. "I'm such a worthless waste of skin. Why did Jeannette leave me? I wanted so much to be her man, to be a father. I'll never know love again, never see a son or daughter laugh. I'll never..."

Ernest tried to run blindly toward the hole's torn edge, so the thunclik tightened her hold on his shoulder and grabbed his waist.

"Calm down," she insisted soothingly. "The more you give in to it, the worse your feelings will be."

"But—"

"Calm yourself!" she said more firmly, then began to sing.

"The sun opens on the mountain so fair, to see the golden gleam!

What joyous feeling we shall share thru' the heart's dream!

Bear your love for divine, trust that trouble is no more!

Suffer not pain of crying, for true courage of hearts not sore!

When the golden bell resounds, its ring will herald Liberty,

To greet again crowns all 'round, and we'll sing Victory!"

The unfamiliar lyrics resonated in Piv's metallic voice like a proud trumpet. The music was exciting, filled with courage and the feeling of shining light. As her singing defied Ernest's despair, he felt his fear lessening, becoming milder.

Piv reached up to Ernest's right temple and pressed a button on the mask. A beam of light stabbed the smoke through like a sword. Ernest reached up to the mask look closer, but decided against pulling it off.

His companion smiled. "Yes, you must *not* breathe the smoke, or you might die from a fear-induced heart attack. If you survived that, your fear would be uncontrollable for week. Come now, the end of the hallway is only another forty feet."

He realized he *had* calmed down. Thankfully, enough that he wasn't panicking or a crying mess. Whatever the smoke was, it had an intensifying feedback, as though fear fed into more fear. To stop this, he had to keep calm and carry on. Piv's alternate biology must have allowed her immunity to the smoke.

"I... I think I'll be okay," Ernest said. "But *why* do we need to leave? Shouldn't we stay to fight the enemy?"

Piv replied while running. "Throughout its history, the Shifting Stones has been repeatedly attacked. But this time, they're probably trying to kill *you* specifically."

"*Me*?" Ernest cried in shock. "Why? What's so important about me?"

"You're vital to Oru-Aural's plan to defend the Shifting Stones, and by extension, Earth."

Ernest was so dumbfounded, he simply stood still to think about it. Just as Piv looked back, another massive javelin struck. The roof behind them collapsed, and Piv pulled him away.

"There's no time for a proper explanation. Follow me to the stormfish!"

She hurried him along. Ten minutes later, they reached some sort of launching bay. He hadn't been told what the transport looked like but expected something that flew among the floating rocks, an aircraft of some kind. Airplane or a helicopter. Blimps would probably be too slow. This was a vicious attack, with artillery javelins thrown about willy-nilly. They needed something fast.

What they saw when they reached the hanger bay was wholly unexpected.

The aircraft was a levitating, mechanical whale, dressed in a scratchy woolen sweater. It looked about as big as the American naval destroyer ships Ernest saw during Boston's Fleet Week celebrations. He would have kept staring if Piv hadn't dragged him to a lowered ramp underneath the floating metal cetacean. Another thunclik waited there, on guard with a heavy crossbow.

The guard gestured to the aircraft above. "The storm-fish's engines are charged, the railguns loaded, and the nav entered! The Prognostication is *truly* upon us?"

"Yes!" Piv called as they ran. "We're going through the Svartfjella Aperture!"

"Svartfjella?" the other thunclik asked as they ran through the stormfish. "Are you sure the human can tolerate the cold? He doesn't have much fur on his body."

Naturally concerned Ernest asked, "Cold? What's—"

Piv shook her head. "Don't worry about it. I already stored adequately warm clothing tailored for your body. You won't suffer frostbite if you keep your face hidden from the wind. Now we must find our rooms."

Despite her reassurances, the need for adequately warm clothing against frostbite spoke of danger. *Much* danger. Just as he was about to ask more, he felt the strange whale ship lifting up. Piv busied herself finding a room for Ernest. Since the airship had left the battle, he had time for him to familiarize himself with it. This type of aircraft was a fighter carrier and strike cruiser—a "stormfish." This particular one bore the name SSDV 64 Silhouette.

Wandering through the craft's belly, Ernest found the first level contained rows of gunner pods. Through a viewport, he could see the towns and scattered forest of the asteroid passing by underneath. The stormfish's accelerating speed surprised him. Even though he didn't feel it moving much now, the sight of the damaged buildings ascended over suggested a flight of 200 or 300 miles per hour. Maybe even *400 miles per hour*. Relative speed was hard to measure against distance.

As he looked back at the attacked hospital, Ernest prayed they'd recover quickly. The people here weren't human but seemed deeply religious. Their dedication could carry them through, but he still hoped those good people would have a minimum of casualties. He felt angry and guilty. Why was he the enemies' target? He didn't even know about this war a week ago. Was he crazy? How would he find out for sure? If he wasn't crazy, *why* would the enemy attack an ignorant human who wasn't involved? His questions would have to wait because he needed time to rest after that mad escape. He enjoyed adventures in books, but never expected he'd be in one himself.

The sleeping berths were located on the second and third levels. The fourth level was dedicated for cargo, mostly spools of some kind of "fuzzy" sheet metal, which held little interest to Ernest. His room had a generously wide window in the ship's starboard side. Wandering through the empty berths, he saw strange furniture, apparently made to accommodate the different bodily forms he'd seen. Some rooms had circular beds like the one he woke up in at the hospital, but there were other varieties. There were also gumdrop-shaped stools, seats that looked like horizontal logs in the air, and chairs with large holes in the backrests. Even with the large holes, the chairs looked comfortable, but those rooms had no beds, only pools of water. Some of the rooms' only furniture were the small tables they all contained.

In Ernest's room, he found a series of cupboards stocked with many books. None of the titles were recognizable because he'd never seen their alphabets, which he'd expect from an alternate universe. Then he noticed a small table with a cookie on it. Picking it up, he was surprised its frosting read, "Eat me." Recognizing the Alice in Wonderland reference, he speculated if this meant to eat it. It looked like any other chocolate chip cookie he'd seen, but with the letters. If he was meant to eat it, that deserved a cautious nibble. So when nothing happened a minute after this, he shrugged and ate the rest.

Then he realized he was wrong to trust the strange cookie of an alternate universe's insane asylum world. So *very* wrong.

Barely half a minute after eating the cookie, Ernest had an intense feeling of vertigo and collapsed. Every inch of his skin prickled. It wasn't terribly unpleasant, aside from collapsing on the floor. That said, everything felt strange, as if each follicle of hair on his body strained ever so slightly to pull its way out of his skin. Ernest's vision became a myriad swirl of different colors, all blending, changing, moving, and shifting into each other. It looked as if everything disappeared into, then out of formless blobs of multicolored oil, or if a rainbow fell out of the sky and washed over him. The colors' vibrancy was so intense the only difference he could see was the color. Nothing had any distinct boundary. It changed so much it was impossible to focus, no matter how he tried. Losing all track of time, Ernest began to panic, but suddenly his vision snapped back into clarity. The vertigo disappeared.

Unable to understand, he looked around. Although he felt any amount of time could have passed, nothing around him seemed to have changed at all. He was still on the whaleship. He wondered perversely whether he should have risked Alice's experience while on an *airship*. Onboard, surely even temporary gigantism would be insanely dangerous.

Ernest sat up and waited to see if he'd collapse again. When he didn't, he slowly stood, then looked at the books again.

The titles were unfamiliar, as expected, but understandable now. *"Legends of Fahiik," "Ekallr and Faith," "Cultural Traditions in Aerth,"* and so forth. Why could he read them now? The cookie? How? He realized the room was marked with slight indents of the walls, which served as touch controls for everything from a cooking station to a viewing display. Rather than exploring the room, he worried about that cookie. Though it clearly helped Ernest read an alien language, he'd feel better about whatever it did to his brain if he could ask someone about it.

After a search, he found rooms specific for thunclik, the first of which had a male. He wore what looked like a full-face motorcycle helmet, except it had a metal plate covering his face, and a white cable stretching from its backside. Continuing into the ceiling, it looked like fiber-optics. He was seated in a chair that looked specifically designed for the thunclik's arachnid chassis. It distracted him from concerns about the cookie.

Even though the thunclik shouldn't have been able to see him, he asked, "Are you looking for Piv?"

Ernest paused to reply, "Uh... yes."

"She's in the room several units behind mine, on this side of the hall. Unfortunately, she's unable to talk much while browsing the COBWEB, but I've already told her you've inquired."

Ernest puzzled on how the thunclik did this without leaving his stall or his room. "Um... what is that helmet?"

"The Synchronized Perception and Integration Directional Relay? It allows me to monitor one of the close-range flanks of this stormfish, which I then send to our pilot. The SPIDR also coordinates the tracking systems for the gunners' defense turrets. Those turrets use assisting guidance coupled with my monitoring data, which automatically moves the turret to the target. In combining this with the gunner's discretion, the target is more quickly recognized."

It sounded like a technology more complicated than he could understand. If it was more easier, perhaps reading one of those books in his room was a better use of his time. The cookie *was* disturbing, but it helped him understand the books. If he was entering an alien world full of unfamiliar customs, languages, culture, places, people, creatures, objects, and history, then he'd need at least a few primers. Books could tell him what to expect, and how to avoid giving unintended insults or compliments, and everything else needed for a place where *humans* are the aliens. But he still wondered why he wasn't presented with this option at the outset.

The first book he chose was a history of how tribal Vungir migration developed into fiefdoms, which then became loosely allied city-states known as the Vorth Republic. Named after the region many of these Vungir settled in, the Vorth Republic lived for mutually unified civility, led by a democratically elected chief. In the use of individual skill or learned experience, they found a healthy balance between teamwork and competition, always reaching for a happier life. There was even a foundational agreement for the protection of this as a philosophy. Though at first, the narrative was dry, Ernest thought the life it described was fascinating. He read the volume regarding the recent history and became concerned the Vorth Republic was being slowly corrupted from within. This apparently started with recent business from the militaristic Grefarn Empire. Ernest found something uncomfortably familiar about this but couldn't pinpoint why.

Halfway through the recent history volume, the ship jolted violently and the sound of projectiles striking metal filled the room. Outside his window, Ernest saw... a swarm of birds? As he concentrated on this, the sight of it made him think of the fighter plane dogfights he'd seen in war movies like *"The Nimitz Phalanx"* and *"Flight of the Nimble Nancy."*

Stunned, he watched the fighter aircraft attack each other. If this enemy really was here to kill him, he wanted to *do* something about it, not simply watch. Dashing out his room, he ran into the hall. Another explosion shook the flying mechanical whale, throwing him against the wall.

More shots struck the sides, harsher now. As the heavier impacts shook the ship, Ernest ran to the storm-fish's bottom level. When he got to the rows of gunner pods, he almost ran into a thunclik jumping into a pod.

"Hey, can you tell me how to use these guns?" Ernest asked. "Anything specific I need to do with them?"

She looked him up and down. "You're Ernest? I expected you to be taller. No, there's—"

Another spray of bullets peppered the side of the flying ship. The thunclik jumped into her turret and took aim. Accepting she had to do something more important than answering his questions, Ernest looked for an empty turret. Most were occupied. Amid the increasing gunfire, another explosion shook everything, even closer this time.

"*Ernest?* What are you doing down here?" Piv ran up to him. He started to respond, but another blast interrupted him and he fell against her.

He began again. "I-I wanted to do what I could to fight back! I don't want to just hide in my room and—"

"They're here for *you!*" Piv dragged him from the turrets' access corridor. "They're concentrating their fire on *this* level now! We need to get you back to the middle of the stormfish!"

"But I—"

"*Don't* argue! We need to get you deeper inside!"

"What?"

Piv shouted, "We *need* you back inside!"

As she pulled him along, Ernest tried to ignore his own questions. Dashing up several levels, Ernest realized they weren't running to his room. Unsure what was going on, he simply followed as the Silhouette shook around them.

Before long, they entered a corridor of rooms with more equipment like the SPIDR. Piv opened a nearby door and yanked him inside. The room's chair was covered with lines and lines of light. There was a pair of wired gloves and some odd goggles hanging above and in front. Bearing a strong resemblance to the ORCC, Ernest was reluctant to trust it.

"What am I sup—"

Piv didn't wait. "Chair, *now!*"

Even as he started toward it, Piv was impatient. She picked his body up, then set him in the chair faster than he could move. Piv pulled down the gloves and goggles.

"Your Earth has finally started using virtual reality simulations, right? Users experiencing a computer-generated reality *inside* the machine?"

Ernest stared at her. "V-virtual reality? Uh... y-yes, but—"

"That's basically what this is. Virtual Reality used to remotely control one of the stormfish's fighter drones, or ROARs. If you understand those two concepts working together, that's good enough. I—"

Another even louder explosion wrenched the ship, staggering Piv. When she struggled back up, she was deeply alarmed. "They've destroyed one of our propulsors! No sleeper cell could have enough firepower for that!"

Ernest remembered she mentioned sleeper cells before. "What do you mean by sleeper cells?"

Piv glared as if he had said something stupid. "They're terrorists who disguise themselves. It's been explained by Earth's news services and governments. The bad guys pour out their propaganda, some idiots believe it and join their side. The sleeper cells pretend they're ordinary citizens, hiding behind their innocent façade, waiting for a signal to strike. But not even—"

Another blast rumbled even fiercer.

"Get those goggles on!" Piv shouted. "These are more than sleeper terrorists. They must've opened a connection to Bu' Zast's Mire of Worms, or—" Suddenly Piv's eyes widened. "They're Ahbis' Paralyzers!"

"Paralyzers? Who's Ahbis?"

"No time!" Piv shoved the goggles at Ernest. "Get these on. We need all the help we can get!"

Without another word, she hurried out. Ernest stared at the goggles, wondering how the technology worked with magic. If, as Oru-Aural had insisted, physics was simply a practical form of magic, perhaps that's why holograms or VR tech worked here; because science and magic were united. Alongside creatures made of living metal with what seemed like a demigod for a ruler. Rather than question it, Ernest put the gloves and goggles on.

The transition from his bodily perception to the ROAR fighter craft was *disorienting*. It felt like his mind was sucked into the fighter craft. If he was seeing status information in a Heads Up Display HUD, with a digitized appearance, this made sense. Somehow, he felt the air around the fighter craft and the launch deck underneath. Almost like his human body was *completely* replaced by a new body. With the senses of a powerful jet.

The HUD had the obvious indicators: power, structural integrity, ammunition supply, etcetera. In the center was a flashing message, "This ROAR unit's callsign is Green-4." Presently, the HUD appeared to start a pre-flight sequence with a rapidly moving progress bar.

After it finished, Ernest felt the launch deck's securing hooks release. A message blinked in the center of the HUD.

"Engines ready. Launch?"

The instant he thought about launching, there was the sound of jet turbines. A few seconds later, he shot out like the vipers of *Battlestar Galactica*. He could *feel* the air rushing past his wings. As much as he wanted to focus on the thrill, he had to focus on the fight. Flying straight into the combat zone, he quickly noticed the HUD highlighted friendlies in red and attackers in blue.

Piv's voice sounded in his ear, "You see that cube display in your HUD's lower left?"

"What?" Ernest asked.

"HUD's lower left!" Piv yelled over the comm, and Ernest saw it. "That cube is a three-dimensional representation of everything around you. You're the glowing dot fading in and out at center. Remember, as your HUD said during startup, your callsign is Green-4. Mine is Fissure."

A quick glance at the cube showed Ernest a blue dot quickly closing in on him from behind. Ernest thought to dive, and the drone reacted. His perspective plunged downward much faster than he expected. The instant pitching dive without warning was *difficult* on his senses, to say the least. But now the blue dot wasn't behind him anymore. Clearly, the drone reacted in real time to his thoughts.

The cube indicated the enemy dot was now the one he saw approaching him! The other fighter made looked like an oily black cluster of tentacles. For all the ghoulish appearance it had, there was no obvious reason why it could fly. As Ernest considered how to attack, twin streams of metal pellets burst from his wings. Shaking off his astonishment, he looked around for his next target, and saw... well, he wasn't sure what it was. The light seemed to bend around a certain spot in the air, as if what he saw behind the distortion was visually warped. The effect resembled the waving, heated air above hot summer asphalt. Confirming his suspicion, another tentacled fighter shot out of the distortion.

Not sure if his voice activated the comm, Ernest shouted. "P—er, Fissure! This is... uh, Green-4! I can see some sort of distortion to aft and port-side of our storm-fish! I saw one of those enemy... *things* fly out of it!"

"Good!" Piv, or Fissure, returned. "Concentrate on the distortion and highlight it in your cube!"

Unsure of how to "think" the drone into doing this, Ernest focused, and a new icon appeared. It was a rotating capital "X" aft of the transport, as he'd described.

As the other thunclik drones closed in on the distortion, something much larger than the strange tentacled fighter things exited the portal. It was an irregularly shaped mass, with a somehow familiar blackened tone, filled with so many holes it looked like a sponge. He didn't know why, but something about it *disgusted* him. More of the tentacled enemies flew out of the holes as it menaced forward. Shuddering from the horrifying unknown quality he could not name, Ernest asked the obvious. "How do we stop it?"

"One of only two ways," Piv replied grimly. "Either sheer overwhelming force or... suicide dive bomb as deep as possible."

Highlighting itself as a threat, the monstrous shape flung dark oily smoke out its nearer holes. As the smoke trailed back to the strangely disgusting mass, the recognition hit Ernest. This *thing* reminded him of rotting meat. The dreadnought seemed *literally* made of death, perhaps to make it as emotionally repulsive as possible. Using the psychological effect to force reluctant attackers to flee from something so abominable.

During a previous warehousing job, Ernest took a shortcut through an alley and found a cracked and forgotten crate. It emitted a strong stench, with flies swarming around. Despite this, he wanted to know what to say to his supervisor, so he opened the lid. If he hadn't seen the rotting steaks' labels, he wouldn't have recognized what it was. He had retched so badly he had to skip out on work that day. But the crate of rancid meat certainly hadn't poured out nightmarish fumes.

"What is that smoke?" he asked.

"That airship is one of Ahbis' paralyzers! If too much of the smoke lands on our transport, it won't be good! Fire!"

Ernest saw a wave of thunclik fighters dive, guns blazing. The rancid meat airship was larger than he expected, twice as big as the thunclik stormfish. As the ROAR fighters dove, the enemy cruiser shot pellets from multiple angles. Some were hit, the drones exploding into fiery balls that collided with the cruiser. But some got through, their bombs ripping the surfaces around the explosions.

Joining the action, Ernest flew in with a second sweeping wave, and pitched the fighter nearly straight down. As he started diving, the "range to target" decreased rapidly. 3,500 feet. 3,400 feet. 3,200 feet. 2,000 feet. 2,700 feet. 2,300 feet. 1,900 feet. The air *screamed* past his fighter's wings. His attention was only for the swiftly growing image of the putrid meat ship, if a ship it was. He'd never expected an enemy to look like that.

As his distance closed to 1,000 feet, Ernest released a bomb from his HUD. Banking hard to climb out of the dive, he felt some odd sense of the fighter's G-force. Even if physically, he was in that chair inside the stormfish, the experience of it suggested he ought to be dizzy to

As the ROAR fighter lifted up, the explosions rumbled behind him. Amid the smoke, he felt something sticking to his wings. It slowed the fighter until it felt like trying to fly through thick mud. The more he passed through the smoke, the more it slowed him down, so much that his climb was shallower than the others.

He saw another ROAR get caught in a sudden updraft of the strange smoke, sending it crashing. If the properties of tar, smoke, and glue were combined, that was this. It seemed to soak up inertia or motion. They needed to attack *differently* than bombing or shooting the dreadnought out of the air.

The smoke. They needed to stop up the smoke.

After remembering Piv's callsign, Ernest yelled, "Fissure, how do we stop that smoke? The bombs aren't enough!"

"Green-4?"

"Er... yes! How do we stop it?"

"You don't have any ideas?"

"No! Why would I? This whole place is entirely—"

"Don't say it!" Piv warned harshly. "Tell us now, what's the *first* idea you have?"

"What do you mean? Don't we need something more concrete than brainstorming?"

"*Stop* doubting!" Piv sounded quite angry now. "We have powerful technology, but faith moves us more than you think. Personal doubt will only act against you here. Now, *focus* about this situation and tell us what your idea is!"

Confused by her anger, Ernest thought about the problem. Gazing down from his altitude, he watched the ROARs darting shortly above the smoking surface. Sweeping side to side as they dodged the sooty columns, he wondered if they could plug up the smoking holes. Even if the damage created debris, the bombs might actually blow them open more. For all the bizarre differences of this situation, the rotted appearance of the holes reminded him of something else. The few times he had forgotten old food in the back of his fridge, his leftovers had never rotted *this* badly.

"Fissure, do you know of plastic wrap?"

"Yes!" she answered. "But how does that help?"

Ernest turned his fighter back towards the stormfish, looking for the launching bay.

"The cargo hold!" he recalled. "Those sheet-metal spools—can we attach them to these fighters?"

"Sheet metal spools?" Piv asked. "Isn't that more like aluminum foil?"

It didn't take very long to attach the spools. Piv told him the sheets were used for the thunclik airships' "skin." When assembling the airships, the sheets were attached to a drone, then it was unrolled while flying around the stormfish's body. Ernest said the description made him think of making a parade float out of a giant roll of duct tape. Shaped like a whale. Laughing, Piv agreed the imagery fit.

Like the thunclik, the aircraft also had metal "flesh." The skin used microscopic fibers to self-adhere to any surface except itself. Ernest recognized it as the Van Der Waals Force. It was strange to see familiar physics and science in this alien place. But he figured if it worked on Earth, it would work here, too.

Soon enough, Ernest's fighter had a sheet metal spool on its backside, ready for "TP-ing" the dreadnought. When triggered, the spring would unroll like duct tape over the enemy ship carrier that looked like a rotting steak. Ernest wondered if holiday leftovers would ever look the same. He suspected again, this might be part of a psychological effect. As he approached, Piv told him she'd be his wingman. A second thunclik would take his other side, with Ernest flying in the middle.

Fortunately, the enemy gunners either weren't trained for close range, or their equipment wasn't capable of it. Immediately after releasing the sheet, Ernest felt a strong tugging as the spool unrolled behind. In a surreal reflection, only a week ago, he was struggling to pick up the pieces of his heart, alone in his apartment. Now, he was remotely operating a virtual reality fighter drone in an alternate universe. Even if this was actually insanity, it was a pretty epic delusion, so at least he was having fun.

As the sheet's sound filled his ears, he felt proud of his idea. Even while the other sounds of battle competed for his attention—occasional fighters being hit, the rumbling shake of the explosions, everyone's attacks mingling—Ernest focused on completing his task. Nothing mattered except staying true to his course. He ignored all else but choking this monstrosity with its own tar-like smoke.

He didn't know how he succeeded, but Ernest completed a lap around the enemy airship. Perhaps it was random luck, unconsciously avoiding the smoke, or maybe God helping him, even *here*. Ernest pushed his drone faster as he flew around and around. Even in the middle of such a battle, the enemy ship kept reminding him of Jeannette's meatloaf. This was strange because she made a very *good* meatloaf. Disgusting as this thing was, it wasn't so much meatloaf he thought of, as it was Jeannette. He *hated* that. As much as he felt mistreated by her, she was not deserving of that feeling of resentment, at least not like this. He didn't want to see this *thing* and think of her.

It spurred him to fly ever faster. He wasn't sure of his exact speed, but he felt a difference as he shot across the underside. Not *nearly* as fast as the hula-hoop time machine, but fast enough to lose track of himself. The edges of his eyesight blurred, while the view ahead of him magnified, zeroing in on the center. Was he trying to flee his memories of Jeannette punching and shouting at him? Or the longing for a relationship that could never happen? Or was he racing to look for a life after his pain?

Why had he been so tolerant of all her wrongs? Of her addictive compulsions and other corruptions? He was glad he didn't want to harbor resentment. But *why* did he want to continue trusting her? The thought pestered Ernest so much it distracted him when he needed to focus on more important things.

"Green-4!" Piv shouted. "Damn it, answer me!"

Though he heard Piv, it took him another half-minute to realize she was calling for him and had been for a while.

"Green-4!"

Ernest answered while avoiding another smoke plume. "Yes, I'm here. What's wrong?"

"We've been calling you for the last fifteen minutes! Your spool has already emptied, and our drones covered half the enemy's ship. We have another stormfish coming to mop up—the Sund."

Ernest looked at the enemy ship. Indeed, it was half-covered, bearing a disturbing resemblance to fridge leftovers wrapped in aluminum foil. Half? How much time had gone by?

"We really don't need to fight this thing now?" he asked.

"No, the other stormfish is only five minutes away now. Your idea worked. The Paralyzer ship is clogged by its own vents. The reinforcements will easily take care of the rest."

He hadn't realized until now, but he felt exhausted. "Uh... how long have I been flying?"

"About six hours without stopping," Piv returned crisply.

Ernest was shocked. "*Six hours?*"

"Yes."

Ernest thought to himself, *But that's impossible! I had to have spent only an hour flying after the spool was fitted! How is it I don't remember?*

While trying to recall the time spent, he approached the transport's launching bay. His only recent memory was flying circles around the enemy ship. He seemed to be missing time and felt absolutely exhausted. Despite this, he parked the drone, then stumbled from the VR chair.

The interface equipment withdrew. The way the bundled cables were organized, Ernest recognized it must have used brainwaves to guide the drone, even for sensory feedback. Maybe it was the same as what a hawk feels, soaring through the sky, but he was too tired for that.

It wasn't terribly difficult to get back to the quarters, though he was so tired he could've slept in the corridor. While getting into the circular bed, he tried again to remember the lost time again, but at most, it only felt like an hour. A couple of hours, if he included fitting the spool onto the fighter drone.

Did he really spend six hours flying himself on autopilot? The drone might have that feature, but surely not him? Whatever happened, his exhaustion felt more akin to being awake for six *days* than six hours. He was asleep before his head even hit the pillow.

What was Ernest looking at now? There was an avenue of trees in full green leaf ahead of him, their vaulted branches turning the park into a cathedral. In the distance, lake water glinted like countless diamonds, while nearby every visual edge was slightly blurred. The colors were so much more intense and vibrant than he remembered. Even Jeanette, her appearance seemed compelling in some new, ineffable way. The inviting smell of barbecue started wafting from the grill she chose. As she lit the charcoal, Ernest hefted the cooler from the car, and paused to look around. This was the picnic area at Amethyst Lake Park, wasn't it?

"Hey, slowpoke!" Jeannette laughed. "Aren't you coming? Enjoying the landscape is a fine thing, but if we're going to eat, we'll need to grill those hamburgers and bratwursts. If you're happy to eat them cold, that's fine but I like them hot. I'm sure my young Joshua wants his hot dogs to actually *be* hot, right?"

Though her son softly laughed next to her, he focused on his robot toy, making it climb the rocks of the abutment. Ernest laughed a little too and lugged the cooler over. Perhaps he was distracted about how to marry Jeannette later. He wanted to ask her about recreating the scene from her favorite movie, "*Joe Versus the Volcano.*" A lot of orange gelatin in the pool, with lights underneath, could be the lava. He was sure his dad would love playing the part of the silly island chief, and their families could all dress up as the wacky Waponis.

Jeannette had such a happy smile on her face. It was a drastic difference from only a week ago, after she drank a whole six-pack of beers. Now she wasn't depressed, wasn't moping about her failures again, or complaining about how much public attention frightened her. The anniversary of their first date was such a happy time that Ernest wished it could just keep going on forever. If only she could be this contented and calm all the time...

As Ernest walked forward, Jeannette smiled at him. Then he realized something was wrong. He watched for a minute before noticing Jeannette's body seemed to "skip." Then he saw young Joshua also repeating his movements. Their limbs jerked, moving back and forth through positions. Even the trees were affected. It was as if they were stuck in a time loop, or reality was suddenly a giant 3D-animated gif file.

"She was quite beautiful. You have good taste."

Ernest spun around to see the man he'd met on his neighborhood road. The man who turned out to be an insane, ultra-powerful master of an alternate dimension, wearing a golden business suit. Aural wasn't present.

"What's going—"

"What's going on," Oru answered "is that you're dreaming again. Normally, Oruaural flits through mortals' minds like hopscotch! Fun, but confusing. You're seeing this because you're still holding onto this happy feeling and don't know how to let go. Even after the wrong she did to you, you keep hanging onto this feeling. Though you can't trust her now, you don't want to hate her. This is right and very noble of you, but you shouldn't hate yourself either, or hold on to this fantasy. If you could make this moment last forever as you wished, then you would be forever stuck in it, a stasis as if you were dead. Life is about moving on to new things and making *new* memories, as much as it is about cherishing the memories you have loved. By the way, your plan to recreate your wedding with the volcano—Oru *likes* it! You're such a maniac! But that's not why Oru is here. This is about what *you* want."

"What *I* want?"

"Well, it is your dream, after all. Aside from Oru appearing, you're the one in control here."

"Me? What do you mean? You're the super-powered Emissary of Madness, aren't you?"

"Yes, but that power only extends over the Shifting Stones. All Oruaural can do in dreams is talk to people.

Oruaural is even more limited here, because Oruaural doesn't exist yet."

Ernest raised an eyebrow. "Your thunclik minions said something about that earlier. If you don't exist yet, how can you speak now?"

"Because dreams aren't bound by linear time. So, despite having no physical influence, Oruaural can help guide you in the mortal world. This is how Oruaural speaks before Oruaural exists! It allows a rather sneaky quality to Oruaural's special talents, or *noesis*, if you prefer the classical Greek. And this does not violate the RULES! Oruaural **loves** it!"

Ernest almost missed the new revelation in Oruaural's insane mirth. Gaping, he asked, "*You* are bound by... rules?"

"Yes." The mad Emissary's face grew angry. "It's the rules that ensure everything and everyone has meaning. But they're *so* confining! Oruaural **hates** the RULES!"

Ernest frowned. "Didn't you just say you love what they do for you?"

"Yesss! Oruaural loves how they also confine Bu' Zast, evil Lord of Blue. Haha!"

"Blue? Didn't you say Bu' Zast is the Emissary of Devastation?"

"Yes!" Oru shouted gleefully. "Oruaural is the Emissary of Orange! It's only natural that Oruaural is the opposite! But enough about one side versus the other. You were asking about the RULES, weren't you?"

Happy to get an explanation, Ernest nodded and waited. Then, he waited longer than expected and groaned. "Do you need me to *ask* what they are?"

"No," Oru said, "because the RULES forbid the discussion of the RULES."

Ernest wanted to tear his hair out. "But... we're doing that right now!"

"Yes!" Oru agreed. "But that's the first one! 'No being, object, or place may examine the RULES without the expressed permission of the RULES.' They have their privacy to think of, after all. Of course, there are the Edicts, the RULES that are commanded by the RULES to be publicly considered. We would ramble away from the narrative if we considered them now, so that's another discussion Oruaural must save for later."

Ernest was quiet, not because he didn't want answers, but because he suspected he might not stop shouting.

Oru continued. "No, this discussion is not about the RULES. Oruaural came here to discuss the next step of your adventure. You should know the most painful and terrible tragedy of Jeannette's life is to not seek marriage. She would deny it of course, because she *did* love you although she wanted to believe she could set the terms. I'm here to tell you that pining for her, despite rejection, is to inflict her pain onto yourself. You cannot find marriage if you hold on to the hope of marriage with someone who refuses it. It is time to move on with your life, to love and romance and all those joyous things! Love is the worthiest adventure! Er... did Oruaural get mixed up? Good! Getting mixed up is an important part of cooking! Anyhoo, when you're awake again, remember you need to relax. Enjoy the tavern. Find out what the general attitudes and feelings are. Get the skinny on the bad people!"

Ernest sighed. "Great, back to cryptic metaphors. I love the cliffhanger."

"*Yes!*" Oru was beyond enthusiastic again. "Oruaural *loves* cliffhangers! Oruaural is ecstatic that you love them, too. Wasn't it *wonderful* how Oruaural kissed you off that roof? Oruaural enjoys hanging on cliffs, but that's Oruaural's nature. Now, it's time for you to wake up!"

With that, Oru hefted a large water balloon and threw it at Ernest's face.

The splash of water wasn't altogether unpleasant. Ernest blinked his eyes and rubbed his face. Piv stood next to the bed, holding an empty glass decanter.

"What?"

"We're approaching one of the Aperture stones, to arrive in Aerth at the Svartfjella mountains. I needed to wake you for our disembarking. Grabbing your shoulder did nothing, so I splashed your face with that water. Sleeping that deeply usually means Oruaural is speaking to you through the dream."

Ernest was still confused how Oruaural could do that if he didn't "exist." Deciding against asking questions he couldn't get answers for, he looked out the window. Their stormfish approached rows of spires, each crowned with a ring of platforms. Most already contained parked airships. The bulk of these were strike cruisers like the Silhouette, or simple transport ferries, but a few seemed equipped for heavy combat.

The smaller cruisers, such as the one he rode, resembled mechanical flying orcas. But these larger combat vessels seemed closer to humpback whales, also wearing "sweaters." Dotting their sides were small turret pods, with heavy railgun artillery in front and back. Ernest figured if one of these was the Sund, after finishing off the enemy dreadnought, the thunclik battleship might've only needed a short hour. Especially if the enemy was already disabled.

As the Silhouette docked at a tower, Ernest asked Piv what to expect next.

"We're going to visit a tavern first before the Aperture."

"Oru said something about that in my dream. Why?"

"Because Aerth is an alien world to you, and torn by unrest," Piv explained. "A massive world war is impending, and if we do nothing, it will be much worse."

"War?" Ernest asked. "What do you mean?"

"What do you mean, what do I mean? I mean *war*. Armies. Soldiers fighting with weapons. Civilians in danger. Some will die. Some will not. Cities attacked, their countryside ruined. Destruction the likes of which—"

Ernest held up his hand. "Okay, okay. I get it. What I'm asking is, why are we stopping in a tavern?"

"Because taverns are places where people from many different backgrounds chat about current events," Piv continued. "You can get important information from books, but if you want the people's opinions, you need to go to the people."

"Books? That cookie? That was *you*?"

Piv grinned. "I left it for you on Oruaural's orders. It implanted in your mind, what you needed to read those books. To give you the knowledge you needed of the food, clothing, cultural customs, weather conditions, geography, histories—and many other things—of Aerth. Since you didn't grow up there, you wouldn't know what is a compliment or insult. The unscrupulous may use your ignorance to trick you to any evil purpose."

Ernest felt both angry and confused. This represented *considerable* foresight on Oruaural's part, but must he truly accept the tampering of his brain chemistry and memory without warning or permission? "But..."

"Yes," Piv nodded, noting Ernest's expression "you have a justifiable reason to feel angry and frightened. Your mind makes you who you are. Nonetheless, Aerth is as alien to you, as you are to it. That cookie transferred vital information to you through the sensation of taste. It did absolutely *nothing* else, aside from leaving you disoriented and hallucinating for a minute. You have recovered and are not harmed. If it helps you feel better, think of it like Star Trek's universal translator, or Douglas Adams' Babel fish. Do you have any further questions or objections?"

Ernest blinked. She efficiently anticipated and explained *all* of it. "Uh... no, I er... I don't."

"Good." Piv sounded pleased. "We should move on to the tavern then. There are several to choose from."

She gestured ahead to the faint outline of the buildings. "The Spry Fly is not exactly a comfortable establishment, but it is one of the most likely places to find stories.

Remember, these people have never seen a human, so they're more likely to react out of fear than sense."

"Wait a minute." Ernest stopped. "If they've never seen a human before, what kind of creature will they think I am?"

"You'll see." Piv grinned. "Come, let's get moving."

As they walked up, the few people outside stared at them, unnerving Ernest. They darted off before he could ask about it.

"I thought you said they were taverns?"

"Yes," Piv said.

"Then why do the buildings look like inns?"

"Because they are both. Now, as I've said, they've never seen a human, so they may react... *strangely*. The residents here aren't completely sane. Accept it, pretend to go along, and we should be fine. I don't know exactly what they'll do or say, but I'll back you up."

Uncomfortable at what *that* might mean, Ernest opened the door. Before entering, they heard all the sounds of idle occupancy inside the tavern—music playing, people chatting, and silverware clinking. But immediately after entering, *all* noise stopped.

Everyone inside stared at Ernest, apparently in fear. Ernest stared back, confused. He wasn't trying to frighten anyone, nor was he violent. Was he misinterpreting them all because of the alien things he saw here? Maybe. Even if mistaken, they desperately shied away from him, as if afraid, though he had no idea why. Earlier, Piv described the tavern as uncomfortable. Now that Ernest saw it, he felt this was being "polite." There were multiple stains, dents, and a few cracks in the walls. The furniture looked weak and splintered, possibly ready to fall apart. He could only guess at how many bar fights had happened here.

Putting it aside, Ernest walked to the bartender, a lanky hornet-like Thvenel. He wondered how such a wispy woman handled unruly drunks.

The Thvenel asked him in a nervous raspy voice, "What kind of creature are you? Are you... a new variety of Ptiris?"

Ernest was surprised again. The memory supplied by the cookie told him a ptiris was not just a casual mention by Oru-Aural. In general service to the Emissaries, the ptiris were the "angels" or "demons" of this world, depending on behavior. From their reactions, these people believed he was the latter as opposed to the former.

What could he tell them? They had never seen or known a human. As he'd been warned, these people didn't know what he was. Would it be easier to let them believe what they wanted, or to try explaining what humans were? If the simplest answer was easiest, then explaining the truth might be more difficult, as he was from an alternate universe.

"I suppose you can call me a ptiris."

The bartender flinched, so Ernest quickly added, "I am not interested in hurting anyone. I serve the interests of..." His cookie memory supplied a word. "I serve the interests of Einheri."

"Really?" Now she was more inquisitive and intrigued than frightened. "Here? Why do you wear that body?"

"Because," Piv interjected, "we are here for the Prognostication of Oruaural's Transmogrification. Isn't that right, Ernest?"

Piv returned Ernest's questioning look with a serious expression of her own.

Recognizing the prompt, Ernest answered, "Yes, I must... ah..."

Piv turned to the bartender. "It will help us to ask you about life in Aerth."

"Of course," the bartender agreed awkwardly, her Thvenel accent highlighting clicking sounds. "I... I can show you to a table. I-is... is there... a-anything specific you wanted to... uh, ask?" Then she leaned over to whisper, "Or do you have a candle counter?"

Ernest asked, "What?"

Annoyed, the bartender repeated, "I said, do you have a candle counter?"

He blinked, unsure of what she meant. Without planning it, he blurted, "Mine is in the store."

"Exactly."

While the bartender led them, Ernest whispered, "What is this Prognostication you're—"

Piv shushed him by pressing a finger to his mouth.

Their table stood next to a supporting post. Its rough surface was covered with graffiti carvings. Most didn't make sense, even after the cookie, but he recognized some of the phrases, slogans, symbols, and caricatures. "Death to the thunclik!" "Oruaural is not real!" "The Grefarn is the *people's* strength." "Master Bu' Zast!" "*I* am my *own* Lord, *I* am Ekallr."

Many of these were crossed out or written over each other, suggesting each new scrawl tried to destroy the previous one. Some were completely scratched away, others merely crossed out. Ernest gestured for Piv. "I recognize what they say, but not *why* they say it."

Piv nodded. "Yes, the propaganda is very diverse here. That 'Death to the thunclik' was probably one of the rebellious Emissaries' sleeper agents, while 'I am my own Lord' may be from an amoral Egoist."

"An amoral Egoist?"

"Someone who thinks about or is *only* concerned with themself. Your culture refers to the self as the ego, the I. Generally, a *healthy* expression of egoism ignores obviously wrong ideas and prefers logical optimism. They still know the difference between good and evil and pursue good. Even to moderate personal expense, because the good is in their pursuit of profit. On the other hand, an amoral Egoist is someone who *believes* they don't need to answer to anyone else's concerns but their own subjective ideas. That the 'Law of the Jungle' as you may have heard it put, is the essence of life. These people often believe that they know best and their personal profit supersedes *any* consequences. They think subjectively, that they can have whatever they want, simply because they want it. Many use the cult of personality, even if the facts of reality don't support their suggestions. The new memory may be difficult for integrating with your mind. You know the Grefarn right?"

Ernest thought for a moment. "That's... some sort of dictatorship, right?"

"Yes," Piv growled "but they don't just run their country with an iron grip, they've also sent agents to spread their influence and spy out secrets. Even here in the Shifting Stones. Ideologically, they are the opposite of the city-state plutocracies, but in behavior they are mostly the same. A few of the plutocrats are exceptions."

From Ernest's cookie memory came a strange recall of events. Protests becoming riots. Battles in multiple places against a government he could never have known. From this, he "remembered" the rioting citizens overthrowing some of their governments. However, instead of devising a new, better way of life, the opposite happened. A small cadre of rioters used the opportunity to seize personal power by manipulating feelings or thoughts.

Among the Thvenel's Grefarn party, power was applied by their new government "in the name of the people." Private merchants were outlawed, as they were seen in this new society as selfish, greedy, overreaching, and apathetic toward the poor. If *any* private property could help the less fortunate, then it should be given to them, without regard for who owned it first. Obviously, those who wielded this unfettered power favored giving to their supporters and no one else. They didn't care if resources or property taken away expansive populations caused *more* poverty. Being "poor" on paper was proof enough, regardless of what finery the new ruling class enjoyed. The "people" were forced to accept in their own name, the new government standard of subsistence. Or else suffering and death.

At the other end of this ideology, were the Allied Plutocratical city-states, also seizing power with manipulated rebellion. Each of these had their own individual name, being allied only in concept. Their new dukes and duchesses were wealthy monopolistic merchants using political propaganda against their old parliamentary democracy. Their big companies provided weapons, mercenaries, and other supplies toward a rebellion. Then, seizing on their personal power, these corrupt monopolies further strengthened their positions by driving away or taking over smaller businesses. Several monopolists recognized this suppression as dangerous, advocating that healthy competition encouraged development towards ever more desirable products or services.

Ironically, both sides of these corruptions fed the other. The Grefarn benefitted from the money of those plutocrats that ignored basic religious morals. The amoralists benefited from the vast numbers of cheap products the Grefarn made by slave labor. When historians predicted a coming abuse of power, people fled to the neighboring plutocrats who still respected moral-driven market ethics. In this context, an Amoral Egoist referred to abusive plutocrats or their fanatical followers, when they believed they "knew best." Some believed their own lies; some merely used the lies toward their own ends. Regardless of whether corruption acted for the "good" of the people or to openly drive out competition, both systems hinged on one thing.

Control.

Managed populations. People brainwashed into believing whatever those in power wanted. Falsified stories of the opposition as murderous, animalistic bogeymen. Changing the language of true stories into completely different narratives, pointing to what they hadn't changed as "proof" of the opposition's corruption or incompetence. Altering what physical evidence they could and eliminating or denying the unalterable. Placing their agents in disguise everywhere and targeting for "reeducation" *anyone* who spoke out. Or simply making their victims disappear.

"What did you want to ask about?" The bartender's question startled Ernest from his introspection.

Ernest peered at her. "What's your background?"

She concentrated briefly. "Well, I'm not sure if you'd understand me. No one has ever seen any... um... anything like you. But if you're a ptiris, you must be one of the nicer ones. You're not trying to eat my flesh or flay my exoskeleton."

A little disturbed, Ernest asked, "Miss, would something that evil *really* be able to pursue such things if they warned you before they did it?"

Her eyes widened. She backed off, repeating her apologies, but Ernest waved it off.

"No worries. As I said, I mean no harm and the thunclik will keep peace. Please, tell us your story."

"Well... um..." She struggled to remain calm, nervous as she was. "My uh... my mother's mother, she told me to talk with you."

"Okay, what's her name? Where is she?"

"Uh..." She was still uncomfortable, but not so fearful now. "She's um... d-dead. Her name is Li' Garner. My name is Li' Rala."

Ernest didn't understand. "Dead?"

Increasingly confident, Rala nodded. "Well, yes. She has whispered secrets to me ever since I saw her murdered by the Grefarn soldiers. She told me to listen for the old countersign, what I used when I fought their new Empire."

This may have been difficult to believe, if not for Piv's earlier warning, especially as humans didn't exist on Aerth. If Ernest was the alien here, and Rala overcame her fear to offer information, maybe *something* told her to speak to him. Was it part of a larger strategy?

"Please tell me what you know," Ernest said. "Is it related to your... grandmother's murder?"

"Yes," Li' Rala answered. "I wish I could go with you to serve Ekallr, but so many of my fears..." She shuddered and went on. "My fears are still with me. Anyway, the Grefarn Empire all began with the rumor that Paramount Gi' Lttras, our high chief, was abusing his power in order to force the poor down. Strangely, the chief's accusers *never* presented any solid proof. It was as if a grand court case was built on hearsay..."

She went on to describe the gradual rise of the Grefarn in the island continent of Ytmir. There was no confirmation exactly of where the Grefarn's ideology actually came from, but many associate it with Urstapin, more commonly known as the "Mad Monk of Fire Mountain." He was said to have been a mystic of the Ash River Monastery, but they vigorously denied ever knowing him, and Urstapin himself lived on the mountainside *opposite* of the monastery. It was never understood how exactly Urstapin was able to convince the Zhee Royals to take him into their confidence, but once there the Thvenel Paramount began relying a lot on the self-declared holy man for advice.

Unfortunately, this bred a lot of resentment from the nobility, many of whose families were traditionally sought after, for advice with affairs of state. Despite the multiple requests by the various dukes, barons, and even a few foreign diplomats, the Thvenel Paramount wouldn't dismiss Urstapin. As anger continued roiling against Lttras' trust of the mystic, remaining loyal nobility pointed to the wisdom and financial successes of the Paramount's father. Unfortunately, Gi' Valtnir's stability was too easily forgotten amid countrywide tragedies. Virulent spreading of convulsive Ersniria, a frightening disease causing uncontrollable spasms in certain individuals, a knifetooth warlord gaining regional popularity by offering communities "protection," against a rival, and severe drought afflicted northern Ytmir.

This ultimately led the angry nobility to seek the ideological strategy of Arxlkarm's cultists, and to convince the peasants that Paramount Lttras was failing them. That Urstapin had no business being where he was, and was using Lttras as his puppet. With many convinced that Lttras needed to be deposed, the final straw was the Paramount's attempt to place Urstapin in charge of the nation's treasury. Over the next few weeks, the people revolted, seizing the capitol in viciously bloody battles. Urstapin was assassinated, but at this point, the attitude was developing new levels of fervor. Angry groups of peasants calling themselves the "Grefarn," led by Arxlkarm cultists moved through each neighborhood, rooting out all opposition.

The Zhee dynasty, known for customs of honor, courage, and creativity, was overthrown. Many people capitulated in fear to the slaughter. Unfortunately, this was sometimes not enough for the Arxlkarm cultists, who kept demanding ever more increasing "proof" of sincerity to the cause. They even attacked some of the nobility who started this, but the cultists had no fear of reprisals, because by that point, they had seized most of the control.

Realizing how the tide was turning, some of the Paramount's loyalists entrenched themselves into forti-fied regions and tried uniting to fight the revolt. Others fled to collections of archipelagos to the east, and pled for assistance from their traditional allies. However, these were already suffering from several conflicts themselves, some battles with knifetooth warlords, and groups sent by the new Grefarn revolt. Most Thvenel countries tended to distrust each other as their aggressive war-like cultures encouraged long histories of conflict, so the neighboring countries preferred not to get involved.

Eventually, those of the former dynasty realized what kind of threat the Grefarn had become, and formed their own coalition. By this point, it was already well past time for stopping the Grefarn's seizure of their country, as the rebels became the new establishment. Thankfully the revolt already used up a substantial amount of resources, so they were stretched thin. Recognizing they couldn't go into war with their neighbors, the Grefarn settled into political containment while making longterm plans. A Cold War had started between Grefarn, and everyone else. Though some didn't believe they needed to be concerned for either side, and if pressed, declared themselves neutral in the dispute.

"They were in that situation when I left," Li' Rala said "but I don't know enough about how things might've changed by now. I've been here for about forty years. Every now and then, I hear a little about new developments, but I can never be sure what is actually true."

"Hmm," Ernest said thoughtfully "even if it's from your... your dead grandmother?"

"A little from her, but not a lot. More from patrons visiting my tavern, so I hear bits and pieces. Some say there's already war, some say it's just rumors."

Piv commented. "That's still a good explanation of how the Grefarn started. This is also part of why we keep the Shifting Stones secretive. Can you imagine the horror might be if the Grefarn saw one of our storm-fish and snuck some soldiers onboard to capture it? We should never allow anything that possibility."

"Yes." Li' Rala agreed. "The only time the thunclik intervene is when there's no other way to improve things for the interests of Oru-Aural. This also means for the good of mortals too. Sometimes we can only figure things out best for ourselves, by doing them and learning from the success or failure. This is what the lessons of history are for."

They spent more time for interviews with the patrons, learning details about personal opinions, the "right or wrong" in affairs of Aerth. Most of the world was in its medieval period, though some people were more technologically advanced than others, jealously guarding national secrets. Globalized trade was plying the seas and wilderness roads. Depending on the perception of politics, every country sought to assure their citizenry (or leaders in power) an edge over the other countries, and exploration was also part of this.

"I remember that guard in the stormfish's launching hangar asking about if I could handle the cold, but this clothing just seems like overkill."

Piv had borrowed the use of the Spry Fly's storage shed, to dress Ernest's body in a full set of an odd white fur. It didn't look like a typical animal hide, but being from an alternate universe, it might be some sort of moss for all he knew. He felt a little sweaty under it.

"The guard was correct." Piv said as she pulled out a tube of some kind of paste. "We're going into the Svartfjella Mountains' Aperture, and it's bitterly cold there. The Vungir are acclimated to it easily enough by their higher metabolism and their bodies' own fur. That's also in addition to whatever clothes they wear. But you're from a climate favoring T-shirts and shorts.

Your body will take the cold as too much of a shock, trust me. If we don't prepare you, then hypothermia would probably happen within an hour or two. Hold still while I rub this on your face."

She rubbed the paste on, and it tickled at Ernest's nose. Struggling but failing to stifle it, he sneezed strongly in Piv's face.

Unperturbed, she explained "This paste is derived from the sap of blackcone pines, and is powerfully resistant against freezing. Whenever its surface is exposed to air, the sap will crust over in an invisible layer filled with microscopic bubbles beyond your count. Basically it's creating an efficient topical insulation, by sublimating at an extremely *slow* rate. That also means I'll need to reapply it every four hours or so. If we keep mindful of that, your face's skin won't freeze, and the suit will take care of the rest."

Given the seriousness of all this preparation, Ernest wondered about the cold even more.

"Just *how* cold is it in the Sv-svarthfell-"

"'Si-vart-feh-yellah' Mountains." Piv corrected. "I understand it's not derived from your native language. I think you might be confused about the spelling, especially when a 'J' is usually pronounced as a 'Y' in this language. The temperature there is probably going to be, by your Fahrenheit measurement, minus fifty degrees below zero."

Ernest's eyes bugged. "-50 F! That's as cold as Antarctica! How do−"

"Actually," Piv interjected "your Earth's South Pole is colder than that, on average. I know you were about to ask about how we'd prepare for it, but we already are. But it won't be cold in the area where we're exiting the Aperture."

"Really huh?" Ernest accented his sarcasm by moving his hand and ruffling the fur.

"Really." Piv insisted. "The Aperture's exit is hidden inside a volcano's lava tube."

"Lava? Wouldn't that require insulation against heat and *not* cold?"

"Insulation against temperatures does both. Besides, your suit has an 'antifreeze' tube network for dispelling temperature extremes. The button for the reservoir's pressure pump is on your right arm's wrist."

Looking down, Ernest noticed a red button the size of a quarter. He figured he missed it because Piv had pulled the suit on his body. Pressing it gave him an odd cooling sensation of the water coursing through the suit, but without getting wet, and he heard the 'sploosh' noise in his ears.

"Now," Piv smiled "I've suited you up, applied the blackcone paste, and I already have the rest of our supplies stowed in my compartments. Let's go to the Aperture."

It was easy to find the interdimensional gateway, because each had a labeled sign with an image. Piv was definitely right about the suit's properties and the black-cone paste. Ernest could only tell the volcano's heat was present because the Aperture kept pouring smoke out of it. There was also a visual "heatwave" effect, like hot summer asphalt. The Aperture created by that disgusting enemy dreadnought had done the same thing. If the distortion effect was caused by the Apertures, he'd have expected the other permanent Apertures to have this too. But they didn't, and several of those had little snow drifts, indicating their exits actually were as cold as -50F or more.

But the image next to this arch was the interior view of the volcanic caldera, with smoke venting from some areas in the hardened lava, and... some lava that was not so hardened. It looked dangerous, but inside a lava tube meant the area that drained itself out, leaving behind a cave. Enclosed as that would be, it offered some protection against the fumes and other volcanic activity.

The Apertures' arches themselves, ranged from twenty-four feet tall like the one in front of him, to stormfish size. They were all made of gold cubes, the sizes of these cubes depending on the arch. The blocks were kinda blurred at their edges in a strange way. Curious, Ernest reached out to touch one.

"No!" Piv jerked him back. "Do not touch them! They're all vibrating in place, powerfully fast. Like Earth's power sanders, but even faster and with vastly more force. If you had laid your hand on it, you would have been thrown backward as if you'd been hit by one of your automobiles on your highways, but first it would have broken every bone in your hand."

"If they're so dangerous, then-"

Piv added "Warnings aren't usually needed, because Oru-Aural's influence keeps most people from touching them. But that's not as important as moving forward, so go on ahead. Into the Aperture."

Remembering the queasiness, Ernest tensed, but felt nothing like Oru-Aural's Aperture. Instead it was...

It was a strange lightheadedness as his vision faded out.

GLOSSARY

Aejlii:

One of the five mortal races of Aerth, they are similar in day-to-day life and physical ability to both fish and cats. With lithe bodies, strong legs, webbed hands and feet, and fish-like tails, Aejlii generally enjoy the sea more than land. Nearly all their tribal villages are scattered along the seafloor, with most structures grown from coral on scaffolds. Although the sea's environment tends to prevent metallurgy, Aejlii are able to make tools from bone, or grow them from specialized corals and shellfish. For the most part, Aejlii villages are agrarian, and most Aejlii are comfortable with this. Due to their skill in swimming, their bodies' natural abilities, and their locations, most oceangoing shipping involves Aejlii at some level. Although Aejlii villages have no centralized government, the largest of these operates their own shipping service.

Like all the other races, Aejlii have a natural curiosity to understand their world, though most are simply content to understand the sea. Aejlii scholars are able to contribute a study of underwater life that other scholars aren't able to. Most Aejlii aren't interested in the politics or other events on land above the water. Aejlii culture encourages a preference for managing their ocean territory as a place for them to coexist, typically by thinning out coral overgrowth, checking for diseases or parasites infecting sea life, and clearing out any masses of rotting carcasses. The differences between sea life and life on land are such that Aejlii usually find inland life difficult to adjust to.

Aerth:

The world where the mortals of the Tapestry's War series live. Socially and technologically, Aerth is in its medieval period. Aerth is analogous to Earth regarding the way in which mortals do or do not accept choices in their lives, and as a setting for the classic struggle of good versus evil. As a planet, it is approximately four times the size of Earth, but with similar gravitational force. There are three landmasses—the supercontinent of Fahiik in Aerth's southern hemisphere, half of which is the Coalition of the Free Kingdoms; at the equator lies the smaller Ytmir, mostly under the grip of the Grefarn Empire; Esplan is mostly an unexplored desert. Between Fahiik and Ytmir is the Icafip Ocean. Separating Ytmir from Esplan, is the massive Tainacl Ocean. The Puroe Sea is the gulf between the supercontinent Fahiik and mysterious Esplan. Aside from some scattered archipelagos, various small islands, and Aerth's polar ice, the northern hemisphere consists mostly of ocean.

Ahbis:

The Emissary of Fear. He seeks to manipulate mortals with fear, intimidation, doubt, and revulsion. Generally, the weapons used by this Emissary are psychological, including illusions projecting the target's worst fears. The servants of Ahbis are known as ghahr and appear as whatever the viewer fears most. Even at death, a ghahr's body appears obscured by a shroud of darkness, like their master. Some wonder if all ghahr are actually multiple manifestations of Ahbis, since he appears the same as these darkness-shrouded forms. The only known difference from their master is that ghahr appear unable to speak. Ahbis' realm is known as the Snare, a place of darkness, fear, and writhing horror. Much remains unknown about this realm.

Amoral Egoist:

People who pursue their own interests above all else. Some will go so far as to seek personal profit from anyone who pays them for their product or service, regardless of whether the customer is the average citizen, or the violent military of the Grefarn Empire. If a majority of these customers demand a particularly evil behavior, then an Amoral Egoist will provide it for the profit from the tyranny of that majority. The dominant trait of these people is the belief that *no* decision is more important than their own well-being. Some even extend this belief against divine judgment, regardless of their personal spirituality.

Examples of Amoral Egoists include dictators, career criminals, politicians, "double-agent" spies, or "sellout" merchants plying *any* area of ideology for profit. Because good intentions may lead to evil results, or formerly evil people may realize the horror of what they did, the classification of Amoral Egoism is hotly argued regarding who fits the definition and why. Many philosophers point to the three dominant faiths' definitions of morality. Generally, it is considered bad enough for a few individuals to actively use amoral arguments to justify their egos, but since this is considered the absence of morality, its threat increases when accepted more by each generation of the population. Then a mob mentality occurs. Entire groups unite in their mutual interest or belief that the group's decisions are the most important, preferring to sacrifice their individuality. Though this ultimately forces the individuals to accept an unspoken agreement, it replaces the individual ego for the sake of a group ego, destroying whatever ideals they originally believed as individuals.

Apertures:

The interdimensional entry/exit portals of Aerth's universe. Apertures allow travel between Aerth and the different realms. Under special conditions, they may even connect to other universes in the Omniverse. Some are permanent, others are temporary. They function based on calculating the various scalar tensors of whatever passes through, using 4-D cartesian coordinate point-to-point positioning, then translating these numerical definitions from one dimensional tensor to the next, in the exiting dimension.

Permanent Apertures require a projection frame and immobility for a minimum of commensurate compensational calculations, and therefore can't be mounted on any vehicle or ship. That being said, certain individuals and types of vehicles can project Apertures, but must calculate additional dimensional tensor values to compensate for all movement.

Arxlkarm:

The Emissary of Deceit and Tyranny. The only Emissary whose incarnated form is unknown, because he or she hides behind numerous other identities. All personal appearances Arxlkarm has used to date have been as a bright and shining orb of light. Communicating with others by sending impressions of thoughts to the minds Arxlkarm targets, it has never used vocal words, but victims have always reported a specific "identity" for the Emissary. The few times there were repeated encounters, Arxlkarm was reported as maintaining the same "identity." As implied in the Emissary's title, Arxlkarm seeks to manipulate mortals into his or her influence by deceit and corrupting the purpose of governments.

Aural:

The wife of Oru, representing the feminine side of Oruaural. Very playful, she has a strong love for practical jokes. While Oru is telepathic, Aural is empathetic, reading emotions but not thoughts. Using this skill with practical logic advised by the thunclik for administrative decisions in the Shifting Stones, has garnered a great deal of emotional support and loyalty from Oruaural's subjects. Aural's name relates to studies of hearing, to aspects of the air, and to metaphysical ideas of auras. This encourages the notion that of the two involved in the pairing that is Oruaural, Aural listens. Though, of course, she shares that role with Oru, in consideration for the ideas and desires of their people. Of the duo that is Oruaural, Oru is more the "speaker" or "doer", and Aural is a "listener" or "receiver." Another note about Aural's name, is the inferred similarity between it and the traditional Latin word for gold, *aurum*.

The Battle of the Southern Hemisphere Aperture Stone:

Taking place en route to the Southern Hemisphere Aperture Stone, it is regarded as a turning point for the history and strength of the Shifting Stones. Before this, defense of the Shifting Stones held its position only with extreme measures, and invading attacks were frequent. At this time, the Shifting Stones were considered neutral in motivations regarding Ekallr because they lacked an Emissary to rule them. The rebellious Emissaries felt this meant the Shifting Stones could be captured and added to the realm of whichever evil seized them. This was, in part, because the military strength of the Shifting Stones needed new tactics, and because the Stones had no official ruler yet, but mostly because Aerth's mortals' behavior favored the rebellious Emissaries.

When Ernest was recruited to become the Court Librarian for the Shifting Stones, the ongoing war for the hearts of Aerth's mortals reached another cyclic peak in favor of the rebellious Emissaries. There was a growing strength of power and might arrayed by evil. The loyal Emissaries were disheartened but held onto the hope of victory. To gain strength for himself and the Emissaries loyal to him, Ekallr let the mortals freely choose how to align. This set into motion a plan that depended on complete unpredictability and the creation of the Emissary Oruaural. Integral to this plan was a messenger, needed to both search for and describe the quest to find Oruaural. Finding someone who needs to be created may sound counterintuitive, but this because of how Oruaural "assumed" the position and identity of Oruaural. However, it was one of multiple events leading to the Oruaural's creation by assumption of the role. Ernest Redsmith was one of the heroes critical to bringing this about. The Battle of the Southern Hemisphere Aperture Stone was meant to interrupt Oruaural's plans before they couldn't be carried out, by preventing Ernest's entry into Aerth. Despite the intense efforts to stop him, Redsmith improvised an effective new tactic for attacking any enemy airships using movement suppression weapons. (See appendix d.3 for additional information regarding Redsmith's "Leftovers" Maneuver.)

Bone Rooms:

A network of hospitals for the Shifting Stones, each is staffed by a mixture of thunclik and mortals. Because of the repeated threats from invasion by the rebellious Emissaries attempting to spread their cults, most medical facilities are built to accommodate the thunclik military as well as civilian use.

Boston:

A medium-sized city to the south of Ernest's hometown of Veil. The two cities are separated by a river.

Bu' Zast:

The Emissary of Devastation. His typical incarnated form is a body made of poisonous slime with an acidic touch. Concerned only with control, eliminating the weak, forcing strength by any means, and exploring all methods of pain, Bu' Zast's single-minded interest in causing devastation and suffering is not only torture. Considered in legend to be the "father" of knifetooth parasites, he actively seeks to cause pain and suffering in any way possible, with a very cruel sense of logic. Because this includes causing mental suffering, Oruaural is especially dedicated to warring against him and preventing Bu' Zast's meddling. Although Bu' Zast understands his schemes are ultimately self-destructive, he believes that in ruining as much of Ekallr's creation as possible, he is achieving some sort of revenge against the Creator. This discourages Bu' Zast from accepting any possibility aside from whatever he's planned. While his behavior makes for an unyielding ruthlessness, it also makes Bu' Zast easy to predict and prepare against.

COBWEB:

A massive database of "cloud" information, accessible by any thunclik. Also, a repository for thunclik personality cores needing a refreshing of memory after a lifetime of experience. To spare thunclik from the memory overload of previous lifetimes, those memories are kept stored in the COBWEB, instead of locally in thunclik individuals.

Convulsive Ersniria:

A disease known for causing frighteningly unexpected spasms in the victims' joints and limbs. A common route of transmission is by the hands of an infected subject, though in most cases the disease doesn't seem to last on surfaces for longer than an average of fifteen minutes. In rare occasions of virulent situations, these mutations of the disease has an extended survival period on surfaces, appearing to last for days, and risk of infection is high. For the physically weak, or even those who have recovered from other more intense conditions, infections have occasionally been fatal. Because of this, especially during virulent surges, panic tends to run high. Even against those who've recovered and gained immunity against furthering transmission. Although the Icadion is considered the foremost location for study and experimentation, microscopes still haven't been invented during the events of "Herald Unexpected," so many diseases' causes are poorly understood. Some theories suggest gloves or other materials that might interrupt transmission of diseases, but these theories are disputed by cases continuing even when the theories are tested.

Cookie of Practical Knowledge:

A method for transferring the understanding needed to survive in an alien world. The cookie transfers knowledge that couldn't be found without living in the subject world for a lifetime. Vital for Earthlings visiting Aerth, or Aerthlings visiting Earth.

Corpus Fusion Chambers:

With bodies composed of metals, thunclik have completely different biology from any conventional carbon-based life. Though parts of their bodies are organic in form and function, their differences in biology require a different form of healing. Many drugs or medicines that help carbon-based life have little to no effect on thunclik biology. Only chemicals that interact with metals have any effect, but they are not openly discussed among the carbon-based, as many are dangerously toxic for their bodies. The most efficient way to heal a thunclik's metal body is with the Corpus Fusion Chambers. A facility for the repair or replacement of the thunclik mechanical parts, and for the location of the chambers.

These are hermetically-sealed, pressurized rooms filled with ionized gases with multitudes of various powdered metals. In the center of each cell, is a mobile platform designed to move in three cardinal directions, up/down, left/right, and forward/backward. On the walls, are rails meant to accommodate 2D movement for a single high-powered laser from each of the walls. The lasers cross their focus on the platform in the exact center of the cell.

When these lasers are activated, their crossing point is just hot enough to weld the ionized powder together with the thunclik's body on the platform. This process is similar to the powder sintering laser-welding process, used for 3D Computerized Numerical Control (CNC)machine milling, but instead of subtracting metal from a mass, it adds metal. The heat of the lasers creates a plasma effect at the lasers' crossing, attracting the ionized metal powder according to the form needed in detailing. The lasers' wavelength may be fine-tuned even to nanometer oscillation. The technology is even capable of 3D printing a brand new thunclik body, minus only the crystalline brain network.

The one part of this process that cannot be produced by the lasers are the crystals and the stored memory of the individual personalities of the thunclik. These are backed up in the COBWEB but must be imprinted into the crystals only after their initial installation. Each personality must be allowed to fully integrate with its body at this point. Upon completion, the thunclik moves the torso and chassis around to familiarize themselves, then to settle the connections between torso and chassis.

Curlequin:

Growing only in the Shifting Stones, it looks like a soft red flower about the size of an average strawberry, but smells, tastes, and is chewed like meat. It has a slower rate of decay than meat, having a nature to grow as plants do, so rot isn't accelerated by time in hot sunlight. Although the Shifting Stones has no sun or sunlight, there is light.

Delirium:

The capital of the Shifting Stones, it is the combined form of the metropolitan spherical Pupil planetoid. Spinning around it like the outer ring of a gyroscope, is the Iris. Though it looks like a planetary ring, the Iris is a solid mass, serving as farmland.

Effecting:

The act of imbuing an object with a new property by altering its subatomic quantum interactions, to enhance the usefulness or ability of a needed talent. This may sometimes generate a completely new ability by using the effected object in this novel way. The vocational career of practitioners in this activity may also be referred to, as effecting, or Effectors.

Einheri:

In the Yalth, a figure predicted to be a messenger, a priest, a king, or a combination of all, depending on the interpretation from the Temples. Considered a foretold champion of Ekallr, he is said to be a bringer of strength and peace in equal measure. Some believe this champion will bring about the perfecting of the Fabric. Some insist this figure is meant to overthrow corrupt tyrannies. Some refer this figure to Ekallr's wishes in bringing back the faithful to the true spiritual intent of the Temples. Still others believe Ekallr already sent this champion, in the form of a previously unknown itinerant prophet named Einheri who brought various elements of this to his local region, which led to the Einherin Church. Among Ekallr's believers, even the Dsunith Faith, which is the most vocal opponent of the Einherin Church, recognizes Einheri as an important prophet of Ekallr.

There were multiple wars over this dispute between the religious faiths, but these have settled down over the past 500 years, though Aerth has still faced wars in that time of a more secular nature.

Ekallr:

Recognized as the unrivaled deity by approximately two thirds of Aerth's population, religious interpretation of Ekallr has developed into three separate faiths.

The Temples of Yalth, which arose from an obscure beginning in the Yalth, an ethnic group of Quastrans living near the inland sea of Osom. This was approximately 6,000 years past the time presented in "Herald Unexpected." This is the earliest known mention of Ekallr, based around a command to spread the word and scripture of Ekallr to any who would listen. The Yalth believe this will culminate with a great high King appointed as the champion of Ekallr, to rule Aerth forever after the Fabric's Perfection has been finished.

The Einherin Church, which developed from the teachings of a humble prophet named Einheri, who appeared around 3,000 years past the time presented in "Herald Unexpected." The early Einherin Church was among a region of Vungir and Quastrans who adopted Yalth beliefs. They believed Ekallr already sent the promised high King, a special champion to speak directly for Ekallr in a personal sense. The regional Yalth leadership dogmatically rejected him, expecting that *only* a figure in pomp and power could be the true representative for Ekallr. Before Einheri was publicly executed by the Temple leadership, he said Ekallr would send him back to Aerth someday, to lead the Fabric's Perfection.

The Dsunith Faith is speculated to be related to Yalth, having developed in the same region. Though historical origins of both are too obscure to ascertain how they may relate. The only other aspect they share with the other faiths are the Edicts of Life.

Although religious wars have been fought in the past, the last 400 years of Aerth have been mostly peaceful, at least with regard to religious disputes. Among the other one third of Aerth, is the worship of nature spirits, Emissary cults (some harmlessly docile, some not), and a growing trend of people rejecting any faith. The Grefarn Empire, for example, fosters an unofficial worship of itself as the ultimate authority over its citizens.

For more specific information about the Edicts of Life, or the various religious beliefs, please read those entries.

The Emissaries:

When Ekallr created his masterpiece of the universe, he created two forms of existence—the physical and the spiritual. The physical is Aerth, the substance mortals directly experience through their bodies. It was always Ekallr's will that the mortals be allowed physical existence, to maintain Aerth as Ekallr's appointed caretakers of the great garden of nature. There is also the spiritual, another existence that is parallel to the physical. Due to the nature of their bodies, mortals are unable to "garden" it according to Ekallr's will. Therefore, Ekallr set a different group of his servants to maintain the spiritual existence. To these, he gave the power to provide inspiration for the messages of Ekallr's will. Though some of these servants abused their positions of power, some did not give in to this temptation and remained loyal to their creator. Ekallr instructed the loyal Emissaries to guard the mortals against the rebellious Emissaries, who sought to ensnare the mortals for their own evil purposes. Such strong division would have led to spiritual war if unchecked.

Thus, Ekallr set boundaries for each Emissary. Some would have a realm as a seat of authority for serving the will of Ekallr; some would be confined, their influence hindered for going against the will of their creator. Because creation has no beauty if it is forced, all had to be allowed to choose Ekallr or rebellion. The choice of free will is likewise given to mortals and must be done with subtlety. For if the options are not presented on the basis of faith, then they are pressured. Oruaural described this in "Herald Unexpected," but the Emissary of Madness must also rely on extra reference sources.

Ernest Redsmith:

The human Oruaural recruited to describe the details of Aerth in human terms and context. Because Aerth exists in a universe completely alien to human understanding, there needed to be a human to describe Aerth's terminology for the audience. Redsmith is also an important figure in the Tapestry War.

Esplan:

A mysterious continent separated to the east of the Fahiik supercontinent, by the Puroe Sea. On this side of its coastline, Esplan's waters are dominated by frequent violent storms, especially as hurricanes near Aerth's equatorial latitudes. In the waters themselves, are strong circular currents whirling in gyres shaped by the rocky jagged coastline of this region, while further out in the Puroe Sea, is a swift and broad south-flowing current. Most of these conditions discourage any exploration of Esplan, but the few expeditions that visited indicated only the coastline had any vegetation, mostly as wind scoured scrubland. Deeper into the landmass, it all seemed to be a vast, sandy desert. Most of the exploratory groups were tasdo looking for new trading opportunities or new settlements for their countries. Disappointed at finding lack of resources or anyone to trade with, low on food and water, the tasdo sailed home. Rumors abound though, that some strange ruins were found as well. Whether this required a hasty retreat or for another reason, isn't known, rumors being what they are.

Eye of the Beholder:

A ring created by Oru specifically for Ernest Redsmith's personal protection. In appearance, it is a gold ring with a large, faceted red garnet. Although one of the very first magical tokens Oru ever created as his test of being half of Oruaural, he had it made only for Ernest's use. To anyone else, it is merely a gold ring with a red garnet. For Ernest, it has three main "effectments." Invisibility against threats, Intangibility for passing through solid objects or allowing objects to pass through him, and Teleportation. It also grants Ernest a fourth ability, the power of which depends on its secrecy. It requires automatic reflexes to activate, but Ernest can use it as needed if he's able to stay calm and focused.

The Fabric:

Aerth's term for the universe in which it and all connecting dimensions exist. The Fabric is one of the universes existing within the larger Omniverse. Only creation's Creator is able to set what exists outside the Creator's creation. Some of the Emissaries' downfalls were caused, in part, by their attempts to move outside the Fabric.

The Fabric's Perfecting:

A period of time foretold in all Aerth's main religions. It refers to a solemn oath by Ekallr to eventually stop any who would attack the righteous. An event in which Ekallr will remove those parts of creation that were corrupted away from the original ordering of existence. Aerth's religious texts suggest that after this has occurred, Ekallr will "close up" reality as in the same manner of rolling up a sheet. There has been much speculation about what this means. The most popular idea suggests it means eliminating any influence of the rebellious Emissaries from trying to corrupt Aerth and the rest of creation, and replacing creation with a new, improved reality, as a perfected existence. Some critics of this idea have suggested it would be filled with interminable boredom, but others refute this by arguing that the aspect of perfection means boredom wouldn't be a problem.

Gakbah:

The prison stone of the Shifting Stones. All new prisoners are told that if they manage to reach the exits, they will be absolved of their crimes and no "record" will be held against them. If someone has been wronged by one of these inmates, the victim will be notified and provided a bodyguard if deemed necessary. Although this sounds as if the inmates are encouraged to escape, it is not so simple, and makes escape extremely difficult.

A reinforcement against evil behavior through unpleasant consequences Gakbah is filled with ever-moving tunnels and a pervasive dust. For the most part, the local thunc-lik's garrison is tasked only with containment. The only intervention for disputes between inmates is an auto-mated focus-perception system, which senses the inten-tions of prisoners. When any inmate tries to seriously assault, rape, or kill any other individual, that inmate is instantly teleported to a randomized new location close to the center of Gakbah, eliminating any progress they made toward escape. Without applying direct force, this enticement toward escape encourages the prisoners to get along with each other, to use teamwork, and to promote more peaceful behavior. If they don't want to lose prog-ress in finding the exits, let alone be sent back to Gakbah, they must simply be civil.

Hahn Stend-Stein:

A Vungir man. Hometown of Testament, in the Svartfjella Mountain Range. He has a strained romantic past with Laeljah Svartvaengr. Though he studied effecting, Hahn was never able to afford the equipment required for it. He pursued a career as an oreseeker instead, using Focus magic to search out the direction of ore veins for prospecting miners. He is an important figure in the Tapestry War.

Ikit:

A fruit grown on trees throughout Aerth. It averages golf-ball size, though there are cultivars of smaller or larger sizes. It looks vaguely like a kiwi, but has a similar taste to cherries or raspberries, with a chewier pulp. The most common color is red, but there's also a full range of all colors, both primary and secondary. Though none are brown, there is a rare example of an ikit tree growing fruit with an even balance of black and white spotting. Flavor and chewiness may vary.

Javelin launcher:

A heavy artillery launcher that fires javelin bolts much like a ballista or crossbow, simply scaled up in size. Mid-range javelins are about the size of the average Earth telephone pole.

Jeannette Vina:

A former love interest of Ernest Redsmith, she matched the physical description of the woman of his dreams. Before his adventures, he felt their five-year-long relationship was the closest Ernest had ever been to marriage. Jeannette was devastated by her parents' divorce, causing her to expect that disaster was more likely than love. However, she still wanted companionship, so Jeannette was torn by the conflict of what she expected to happen, versus what she wanted.

Knifetooth host:

The bodily hosts of the knifetooth parasites, these are people who have been infected, either by choice or by force, with said parasites. Because the parasites mutate, their host bodies develop beyond their natural abilities and weaknesses—a strong temptation of power. Most infected people develop aggressive tendencies while losing intellectual ability. A development of force paid for by a loss of intelligence. This encourages an idea among many hosts, especially those who choose this life, that if they can seize what they want by force, they *should*. For this reason, and for the parasites' origin legend, cultist following among hosts is strongest for Bu' Zast.

Though some hosts prefer using their personal power only for their own ends, most are still intelligent enough to recognize strength in numbers. Most knifetooth hosts find the temptation for extraordinary strength extremely difficult to resist, and often serve as gangs of marauders for host warlords. If the marauding gangs haven't taken to pillaging, violently assaulting or looting a community, they'll threaten complete destruction if their demands aren't satisfied, usually in tribute of material goods, or youths for new hosts. Of course, in addition the temptation of power, some give in their parasites' natures because of the societal stigma caused by fear or loathing of the parasites, while some hosts manage to resist the parasites and remain decent members of their communities.

A widely discussed legend suggested Bu' Zast created the hosts by cutting off one of his own hands and changing it into the abomination. While at his lair, his cultists performed their manifestation ritual, and Bu' Zast appeared as a darkly armored warrior. He offered them a promise of great and *terrifying* power, at a cost. Bu' Zast told the other cultists to seize the supplicant who accepted.

While they held the supplicant fast, Bu' Zast cut off first his own hand, then the cultist's hand. Bu' Zast dropped his sword to grab the cultist's bloody hand from where it fell and replaced his hand with the supplicant's. Using his dark power, the Emissary of Devastation transformed his own bloodied hand into a knifetooth parasite before their eyes. With the supplicant's hand, now a part of Bu' Zast, he cut open a hole next to the supplicant's heart. Ignoring the cultist's screams of pain, the embodied evil shoved the parasite deep into the wound, turning the supplicant into the first knifetooth host.

The Emissary of Devastation commanded him for the sake of eliminating the weak, to spread the parasite's larvae to new hosts upon maturation.

Knifetooth parasites:

The knifetooth parasite is one of the most insidiously dangerous creatures known to exist in Aerth. The parasite is believed to have been personally created by Bu' Zast for spreading his influence of force and corruption of power.

Though Earthlings might think of this creature as an oversized earwig, it is a threat not to be taken lightly. The pincers capable of cutting through nearly any bone, the aggression-influencing chemicals they secrete, and the sacrifice the hosts make of their intelligence, all allow the parasites to appeal to a violent lust for power.

When finding a potential host (held immobile through sleep or against the subject's will), a parasite pushes its tail against the skin—or depending on the host's species, scales, fur, or chitin—and oozes a viscously thick fluid. This is a powerful anesthetic, absorbed by osmosis, allowing the parasite to avoid disturbing a sleeping target, and even powerful enough to suppress the pain from the initial use of the sharp, bladed mandibles, or to walk onto the surface of the body to find a more preferred spot for infection. As it slices into the body's flesh, the parasite's mandibles secrete more anesthetic to suppress the pain that would otherwise wake the target as the wound was cut open. This anesthetic disinfects the wound to prevent infection. When the wound is sliced open and deep enough, the parasite turns the mandibles out, inserting its tail instead. If it is able continue, the parasite's tail exudes another drug that promotes a strong growth of the bodily tissue around the tail. This allows the parasite's tail and body to integrate further with the host's body, while healing the wound.

This drug also promotes the host's body to grow blood vessels to connect directly with the parasite, giving it the sustenance of the body, while also allowing the parasite to distribute its steroids into a localized growth of muscle. The drugs interfere with most of the neural connections in the host's brain, while amplifying the neural connections associated with aggression. In a completed infection, the host's body grows around the parasite's body with an apparently seamless connection, with only a bit of scarring to mark the transition from host to parasite. The parasite's sharp, bladed, pincer-like mandibles protrude from the host's body, ready to bite reflexively and slice at any other body. The mandibles ignore those the parasite recognizes as other hosts' bodies, except for the parasites' breeding season, in which they exhibit a twisted, dark affection, inter-meshing their mandibles between each other.

Hosts determined to avoid becoming the stereotypical monsters most Aerthlings think of as knifetooth hosts, may seek out help in surgical removal of the parasites. However, some parasites integrate themselves near major arteries or nerve bundles, which prevents their removal. A common solution for hosts refusing to submit to their parasites' influence is to mix into their food a carefully measured dose of plateback scorpion venom. This prevents the neural drugs of any remaining parasites from affecting their hosts' intellect or aggression, and to neuter their parasites from breeding. These hosts also have their parasites' mandibles filed down so they cannot cause injury in normal daily social life, though they may still face an awkward stigma for harboring the parasites. For more specific information about the plateback scorpion, please read that entry.

Laeljah Svartvaengra:

A Vungir woman. Hometown of Superstition Spires, in the Svartfjella Mountain Range. She has a strained romantic past with Hahn Stend-stein. She studied herbal medicine to pursue a career as an apothecary and apprenticed with the town doctor. She is an important figure in the Tapestry War.

Magnetic neural network matrix crystals:

A peculiar crystal carefully guided through its polarization growth, these are the computational brains of thunclik. They have a fluctuating quantum charge, allowing for an unusually dynamic magnetic field. Unlike most other magnetic fields, which have a dualism of polar charges, these crystals have three stable polarized charges. These "tripoles" have a positive charge, a negative charge, and a third which combines both. The unusual nature of these blue-green crystals allows for selective types of electric circuits and current flow when multiple crystals are clustered together. An exclusive quality of the crystals, is to create stabilized electrical charges and continuously cycling patterns of current. These localizations might be thought of as partitions of the thunclik brains, such as the divisions in mammalian brains, but not physically separated, only partitioned by the extant of the currents' flows.

These qualities allow the crystals to store memory, computing input/output, even for spontaneous decisions or reactions, and are foundational to the thunclik personality matrix cores. The crystalline brains of the thunclik.

Map of Tapestries:

Ekallr's grand plan; his design for all of his creation. Every thread represents a being's life. Every woven crossing is the interaction of those lives. Some are tangled, worn, and faded. Some are stitched, strong, and bright. The entirety of the larger picture can never be seen up close, only small parts of it. The vastness and complexity of its beauty is so immense that the Tapestry can only be completely comprehended in Ekallr's throne room. Even there, some symbols on it are understood only by Ekallr himself. The height of Aerth's Great Spiritual War reached its greatest turmoil when a fragment of the Tapestry was torn and stolen by several Emissaries. The war was turned back for Ekallr's favor when the fragment was set back in its rightful place.

Marbles:

A widely used monetary unit for the Shifting Stones, various other realms of the Emissaries, and much of Aerth. Despite appearances, these glassy orbs are not glass. They are spherically cut crystal, or gemstones.

Mire of Worms:

The personal realm of Bu' Zast. A hellish dimension of fiery lava, smoke, noxious gases, dust, various forms of torture, suffering, and deaths. Mortals usually associate only three feelings with this realm, an emotionless apathy, the only emotion derived here is the victims' fear, or the sadistic pleasure Bu' Zast and his sociopathic minions feel from causing pain. Although the central area of Bu' Zast's soot-covered fortress is surrounded with a vast lake of molten lava, the outer shores are an ash-covered muddy swamp filled with a wormy muck that has no known bottom. This muck gives the region its name, as this boundary is the only part of Bu' Zast's realm any mortal has personally seen and returned to tell the story. Additional details have been described by religious visions, the other Emissaries, or their servants. Though Bu' Zast has other minions here, the most common are his knifetooth hosts, some of which have let themselves degrade into little more than animals. For more information on Bu' Zast, the knifetooth hosts, or the parasites, please read those entries.

Momentum Negation Chair:

A technology used by the Shifting Stones to reduce inertia as much as possible. The chair works by temporarily matching its occupant's body, as a whole, to the mass and density of the chair. Thus, the occupant's body resists the effects of inertia as easily as the chair. The body doesn't get flung about, nor does it lose consciousness from the G-forces pushing the blood away from the brain.

ORCC:

Also known as the Observational Relativistic Chrono Centrifuge, it is a massive time machine composed of twin bronze hoops as large as a small moon, spinning in directions relatively opposite to one another. Contrary to many ideas in science fiction regarding peculiar devices that manipulate time in some unexplained way, this machine uses the relativistic effects of physics at the speed of light. It is not known exactly what happens to objects moving so fast, but rigorously examined mathematics suggest that the effects of time relative to existence outside of that velocity slows down to the point of stopping. Clocks taken onboard high-speed jets, or sent into orbit moving at over 17,000 mph, have consistently become slower than the exact same devices at rest. This proves that time *does* slow down for the subject the faster they move. This same set of physics also suggests that if the subjects could observe the sight and velocity of each other moving, then they would see each other moving through time. But this would require both observers to move relative to each other at a minimum of half the speed of light. Their observational relativistic physics would have a cumulative effect on each other. Although past the speed of light, they wouldn't see the other's present location, but would see the location of where the other had *been*. With this motion powered by a micro-sized black hole, it also uses frame dragging to amplify the relativistic physics. All of this is made possible by the relativistic observational effects of a complete awareness of one another's motion. Any distraction from this will cause a severe loss of control and chaotic variables to affect the velocity.

Oru:

The husband of Aural, representing the masculine side of Oruaural. He has a difficult logic to follow, applying multiple words that have similar spellings. He often speaks with "plays on words," such as the reference to Lincoln during Ernest Redsmith's first encounter with Oruaural. Even relating the phrase "play on words" to the literal presentation of a play, as if words themselves are the actors and actresses. While Aural is empathetic, Oru is telepathic, reading thoughts but not emotions. For this reason, he works out much of the practical application of policy for his subjects. Oru's name also relates to the act of speaking and to spreading ideas in speech. This encourages the notion that of the pairing that is Oruaural, Oru speaks. Though of course, he shares that role with Aural, in consideration for the ideas and desires of their people. Of the duo that is Oruaural, if Aural is a "listener," or "receiver," Oru is more the "speaker" or "doer." Another note about Oru's name is the inferred similarity between it and the traditional Latin word "Oris." Etymologically, this has become the transliterated word for gold in many other languages.

Oruaural:

Although referring to a paired couple, specifically Oru and Aural, they both consider themselves one whole person, not two. They insist on being referred to as one person but having two different personalities. Distinctions are made only when differences explain more clearly what Oru and Aural are. This reference to the pair as one person even appears in the name Oruaural, as a portmanteau of "Oru" and "Aural", respectively.

The Emissary of Madness. Assigned to guide the insane back to sanity, or to serve Ekallr in providing protection and/or containment of the disordered. In this, the Emissary of Madness seeks to treat mental instability, or to minimize, as much as possible, the suffering caused by insanity. For this reason, Oruaural is the polar opposite of Bu' Zast, Emissary of Devastation, who seeks to *cause* insanity, especially of the darker kind.

Known for an extremely unpredictable nature, Oruaural has a peculiar dual personality. A caveat for this book's audience, if you have not already understood this, is that to truly understand Oruaural, you must be warned that Oruaural is *exceptionally* confusing. *And* unpredictable. Hence, Oruaural's need for Ernest Redsmith. Although Oruaural's duality is often referred to as one character, the duality is literally expressed by the coupling of Oru and Aural. These two personalities may be considered individually different characters themselves. For more information specifically about Oru and Aural, look for those entries.

Like all the Emissaries, Oruaural's presence in their personal realm allows them tremendous power to defend against invasions from enemy Emissaries. Should they leave the Shifting Stones, this power begins to wane. Oruaural's power will wane even faster if they try to visit another Emissary's realm.

Oruaural is especially unusual for being the only Emissary who wasn't created at the same time as the rest of Aerth's universe. Ekallr prepared a plan for introducing Oruaural when he was needed, referred to in the Prognostication of the Golden Transmogrification. For this plan to proceed correctly, Ekallr's enemies had to believe nothing could stop them. Still, the prophecy was there to give the faithful hope, for the sake of the strength that hope gives.

Paralyzer:

The "strike cruisers" of Ahbis, they often appear in illusory form as whatever the viewer finds most repulsive. Armed with vents of a smoke weapon similar to the whelming variety, but physically restraining rather than emotionally dangerous. Used often to slow or even stop its quarry. Before the Tapestry War, stopping a paralyzer dreadnought required suicidal dives with the ROAR fighters, or concentrated heavy railgun fire from three or more stormfish. Add duct tape maneuver reference

Paramount:

A position regarded as the political and military leader among the Thvenel nations. Some are compared to kings or queens, mostly unaffected by public opinion, while influenced by high chivalry in Thvenel culture. Some are elected by a vote taken every seven years. In these countries, the Parathon political system relies heavily on two methods to interpret their citizens' decisions. The local dukes or duchesses of a parathony collect their peoples' votes up to a specific final deadline, then carry them sealed to their central hive and open the package in sight of everyone else. Then a tallying commission counts these votes, all still supervising each other against corrupting the vote total. A year later, the eighth in their election cycle, their government collects a national popular vote from an evenly distributed number of counting districts. The comparative number between the averages of both is analyzed, and the largest number for a candidate is the new Paramount. Local dukes or duchesses inherit their positions, but may be voted out during elections or at any time a threshold percentage votes for it. Likewise, for paramounts or other positions in Thvenel governments, the exception being the authoritarian Grefarn Empire.

For more information about the Grefarn Empire, please read that entry.

Piv:

The thunclik assigned by Oruaural to be the personal guide and bodyguard of Ernest Redsmith. She has the distinction of being the first thunclik for which Oruaural ever used the memory transfer process to create a personality core. For this reason, she's able to have a prescient awareness of events relating to her and Ernest.

Plutocrat:

An individual who uses a vast amount of wealth to rule over a population and collect more wealth. Usually passed along through the generations by inheritance. Because of the incentive to maintain this power or influence by wealth, a usual trait among plutocrats is amoral Egoism. Even though some of the plutocrats planned for social organization with genuinely good intentions, the planning relied entirely on control. These resulted in small oligarchies, each running their states as "company towns," with their systems dependent on controlling their citizens' lives. This breeds a natural resentment when such forbidding enforces uniform rules for all the populace or eliminates foreign products, regardless of their superiority to the plutocrat's products. Concerned by power controlled by an unwillingness to allow independent employment or business, many fled. Those who remained were too poor to travel or were unwilling to give up the sentimental connections to property they still owned.

Among the plutocrats who exhibit egoism, even the amoral, some realized their populations' riots were due to the suppression of competitive choice. That if the populace is allowed to make their own decisions about their lives, they'd be more content, meaning civility born more of practically mutual agreement than of morals. The problem with this is that it still trended toward a mix of evil vices among the good, when these people forgot what was important about the understanding of right and wrong.

Ptiris:

The entities Ekallr created to populate Aerth's metaphysical dimensions. Although not directly obvious to mortals, they exist in the reality parallel to mortals' physical reality. Some believe that mortals affect them, as they affect mortals. Some do not share this idea, or even believe mortals do not exist.

The Prognostication of the Golden Transmogrification:

The nexus of thought will mix with the nexus of emotion. The Shifting Stones will be shattered, divided, warring against itself, and face its greatest foe. Realize thy strength is found in completing the union, question it not. The battle will destroy. The dead will live. Justice will win the day. Thy herald is the man unexpected even of himself, unknown to Aerth.

This is the prophecy foretelling the events of Oruaural's appearance. In "Herald Unexpected," the title implies the appearance and narrative order of the prophecy. Central through this, along with the saga, is the looping causality narrative. A quest to prevent corrupting destruction by sending heroes through time to find a power to defeat the evil, and with that power, give the quest to the heroes.

Quastran:

One of the five mortal races of Aerth, they are similar in day-to-day life and physical ability to crabs. This inspiration is also reflected in some aspects of their cultural traditions. Physically, their bodies are shaped like partially-squashed balls, with three legs and three arms. Although Quastrans are amphibious, they have little to no swimming skill. Quastrans are armored by a hardened exoskeleton. Most of their countries congregate along Aerth's coastlines, or even the shores of freshwater lakes. The necessity of saltwater for Quastran biology is bypassed by using a high amount of salt for individuals living away from the sea. The strongest of all Aerth's races, they tend toward lives in construction, mercenary work, or other vocations requiring strength. Because of their natural traits, few of the Quastran nations have been attacked. While some Quastrans pursue their lives as mercenaries or as soldiers defending their homelands, most prefer to avoid aggression. For this reason, Quastrans generally see fighting or military action as only necessary for defense, preferring isolationist politics.

Quastran architecture is reminiscent of large shells, but built of clay, stone, and wood. They often use blocks or support beams larger than themselves, simply because the tendency to overbuild is easy for them. This promotes an erroneous idea that Quastrans are "showoffs" for their strength, which most Quastrans find amusing, with little interest to correct this.

Quesa Mesa:

A popular nationwide chain of fast-food restaurants on Earth, serving Mexican-themed meals. It was at one of these that Ernest and Jeannette met for their first date. This event on September twenty-third indelibly imprinted on Ernest's memory, and with it, the location.

Restoration Ceremony:

Every year, there are a number of residents in the Shifting Stones who recover from their mental disorders. Some prefer to quietly celebrate this in their own way, but some want to celebrate it with a party. As the Emissary of Madness, Oruaural publicly supports both approaches to this, encouraging a recognition of sanity as a need for pursuing life according to Ekallr's will. Oruaural provides a limited set of supplies for those wishing to celebrate their stabilization in private and may even personally appear if asked for. For those wishing to publicly cele-brate, Oruaural hosts this in the Devotion of Aspiration, a hall so massive the ceiling is obscured in shadow.These are a massive feast open to sane or insane alike, for the happiness of those people returning to their loved ones in Aerth. Occasionally, there are attempts to ruin these celebrations, from narcissists seeking attention, to more violent invasions from the other Emissaries. Oruaural refuses to yield to these destructive efforts against celebrating sanity.

ROAR:

A Remotely Operated Aerial Response craft, these generally serve as the average fighter aircraft support for the stormfish airships. Thunclik usually operate them with direct cable connections, though VR interfaces and brainwave sensors may also be used. The connection between the operator and the ROAR's body is so complete, the pilot will feel as if they have literally been transformed into the ROAR, even sensing the air rushing against "their" wings. With speeds cruising up to 2,000 mph or more, these VR-controlled drones are able to endure such punishing maneuvers they seem to defy expected aerodynamic physics. They fly by forcing air into a pressurization chamber, which then ionizes it with intense electromagnetic fields, transforming it into a room-temperature plasma. The engines' main thrust power is projected from the vehicles' rear, but there's also multidirectional VTOL engines mounted in eight different locations on the drone. These may be rotated to any orientation within a 45-degree angular conical range-of-motion zone, the point of this being the engine itself. Because of the need for an extreme high performance from its engines, the ROAR has an operational period from as short as an hour, to a maximum of six hours. If they are sent long range, it must be by a carrier Stormfish airship.

The RULES:

The conditions governing the existence of all reality and the interaction of all created beings within it. Expressed in subsets of the laws of physics, of moral behavior, of common-sense logic, and of instinct, there are many, in number and variety. They are complex, sometimes one RULE affecting another in one instance, and being reversed in a different instance. Only Ekallr is able to finalize the RULES, or make ultimate judgments about them, since he created them. Even though they have a different nature than that of mortals, both the Emissaries among the ptiris and mortals are governed by it. Appeals for judgement of a situation possibly affected by the RULES may be sent at any time by anyone. The Emissaries' purpose with regard to the RULES, is to apply them to those areas of creation they are allowed to administer to and to make subsidiary judgements for situations in creation. Depending on how they affect situations for mortals, ptiris, or even reality itself, judgements on RULES may be given immediately, or may be delivered later on. The appeals sent for this may seem simple, but given what the RULES affect they are often underestimated. Ekallr has provided explanations of the RULES through examples found in cause producing effect, in the conscience, in nature, in demonstrations of themselves, in the subconscious, and supporting clarification in religious texts. When someone asks, "Why does that/it happen?" even if they don't know it, he or she is asking for the RULE affecting the situation. Regardless of how this may sound, free will is the one thing that is *not* affected by the RULES, but the consequences of those decisions *are* affected by the RULES. Every decision or choice of free will has a consequence, even if the decision or choice is inaction. Some consequences require little need for concern, and some consequences affect existence itself, in ways beyond average comprehension.

Although the rebellious Emissaries reject the subservient authority they would have to the RULES, the nature of their existence is still dependent on the RULES. Because of this, they constantly look at the RULES for loopholes or exceptions to get what they want, actively promoting these loopholes among the ptiris and the mortals. Each rebellious Emissary has their own differing idea of how the RULES should be implemented, or even of how to replace the RULES with their own version.

Shieldscale Formation:

A thunclik defensive maneuver in which a group of thunclik interlock their shields and synchronize their forward movement. By keeping their shields locked together, while carefully moving at the same speed with weapons pointing out between the shields, the group becomes an armored unit capable of shrugging off much heavier enemies. It also helps that thunclik bodies are literally made mostly of metal.

The Shifting Stones:

Personal realm of Oruaural. Sometimes referred to with respect as the Sanctuary of Ekallr's Providence. Sometimes mockingly referred to as the Asylum of Ekallr.

Serving Oruaural as a personal realm for guiding the mentally disturbed back to sanity, the Shifting Stones seems to challenge sanity itself. Shaped like a cluster of asteroids, they are constantly drifting through a massive sphere of atmosphere and are covered with various wild environments. Travel between the stones is provided by stormfish airships dedicated for ferry use.

Although some of the insane residents will occasionally have disputes with each other, their mutually surpassing respect for Oruaural and the thunclik helps them live in peace. Not all of the residents of the Shifting Stones are insane, but are family or close friends of the disturbed. Some residents are perfectly sane, but sought the Shifting Stones because it is a place disconnected from most of Aerth's problems. Others simply liked the fantastically unusual features mentioned in the stories of the Shifting Stones and found their way in. An important note is that the permanent Aperture locations for the Shifting Stones are mostly kept secret. For the intention of keeping the secrets of the Shifting Stones safe from the rebellious Emissaries' cultists or minions. On the other hand, the insane of Aerth are guided to the stones by Oruaural appearing in their dreams. This is the origin of the phrase, "whispered to by Oruaural."

If someone does manage to enter an aperture of the Shifting Stones, the aperture automatically sorts this out based on the subject's state of mind or intentions. For more general information specific to Apertures, please read that entry.

The Shifting Stones' Automated Exit Classification System determines the location of where or under what conditions the new visitor appears. Four examples are:

1. Subject is a mentally disturbed person who has committed frequent murders of innocents "conspiring" to kill him. Subject doesn't want to kill anyone except those "attempting" to kill him. Exit is a containment and observation outpost guarded by thunclik. Subject is detained for one month, has psychiatric sessions with a thunclik specialist, then is released under a warning that if he has a complaint, he *must* report it to the local thunclik. If he behaves violently, or commits other actions of ill intention, this will be considered a crime and investigated. To avoid confinement at the prison stone, he should let a dispute be settled by proper authorities. A thunclik may accompany the subject

personally as they acclimate, before resuming his or her usual duties.

2. Subject is an individual who is *certain* that gold and butter are the same substance. Subject is "harmlessly crazy." Exit is a dedicated unrestricted public access area with no other concerns applied to subject.

3. Subject is the wife of a man who entered earlier, when he started hallucinating due to a brain tumor. Subject is perfectly sane, merely having a strong desire to be with her husband. Exit is a dedicated unrestricted public access area with a notification sent to the local thunclik garrison to show the woman where her husband is being cared for, then to take questions on planned decisions.

4. Subject is a knifetooth host of the Bu' Zast cult who seeks to spread knifetooth infection and violence among the Shifting Stones. Subject is violently insane. Exit is a directly immediate appearance at one of the prison stone's new arrival containment cells. Notification is sent to the thunclik garrison guarding the prison stone. The parasites will be surgically removed as much as possible from the subject's body. Then he will face years of mandatory sessions with the thunclik psychiatric specialists, while under confinement. If he has demonstrated he no longer believes Bu' Zast

should be his master and no longer wishes harm to others, then the subject is released. They are warned of surveillance and that crimes will be investigated. If he is found guilty, it will result in his confinement again.

For more information on prison stone Gakbah, please read that entry.

Sleeper cells:

Citizens of a country or society that have been brainwashed by foreign propaganda into believing their native or adopted country or society is somehow evil. They pose as average citizens, but are radicalized to believe that eventually a cooperative effort of violence is the *only* solution to a problem, even if the authorities there are not violent. Although this may have short-term effect on what they want, most find the long-term effect becoming the opposite of what they want. Many in Aerth are part of paramilitary groups headed by knifetooth warlords, or sponsored by dictatorships like the Grefarn Empire.

Southern Hemisphere Aperture Stone:

Serving as a major transportation hub for all Shifting Stones travel to Aerth, it contains twelve Apertures. Because of the importance this hub has in affecting both the Shifting Stones and Aerth, the thunclik have strong fortifications here. Only Delirium has more dedication for its tactical fortifications. For more information about Delirium, please read that entry.

The Spry Fly:

A popular tavern serving travelers visiting the Southern Hemisphere Aperture Stone of the Shifting Stones. Intensely regretful of the time she served in the Grefarn's Shining Star rebellion, the tavern owner who greeted Ernest Redsmith was Li' Rala. The betrayal she suffered in the fighting was so bad she still suffers PTSD from it and has a strong sense of nervousness. When she realized the Grefarn were using the deception of good intentions to hide the grievous flaws of their ideals, Li' Rala turned to the royalist Elan. Unfortunately, by that point in the rebellion, too many Thvenel had given their hearts to the Grefarn, and the Elan were losing. In despair, the royalists became an exiled government, fortifying themselves in a mountain valley within the natural terrain. Li' Rala sought peace in the Shifting Stones and started her tavern.

SSDV 64 Silhouette:

Shifting Stones' Defense Vessel Silhouette #64. Resembling a flying orca whale, this airship is a light cargo transport and fighter drone carrier. Armed with two heavy artillery railguns in the bow and four medium railguns in aft. Has a top speed of 450 knots, reduced to 200 knots during storms or other rough weather. The airship that Ernest and Piv used to leave the Shifting Stones. A lightweight carrier of VR-controlled fighter drones with invisibility camouflage, this ship is optimized for quick dashing sorties, reconnaissance, and ambush missions. It was on this airship, during a now-celebrated battle, that Ernest innovated the "duct tape attack". For more information about the Battle of the Southern Hemisphere Aperture Stone, please read that entry.

SSDV 108 Sund:

Shifting Stones' Defense Vessel Sund #108. Resembling a flying humpback whale, this airship is a heavy-impact artillery battleship class with armor-piercing railguns. Like all battleship class stormfish, it has all sides armed with heavy railgun artillery—four in the bow, another four in the aft, two on belly, two on dorsal, two on port, and two starboard. Between the heavy artillery, smaller rapid-fire turrets pepper the hull. Has a top speed of 302 knots, while requiring stabilizing maneuvers in stormy weather, slowing the airship to an estimated 100 knots. Towards the end of the now celebrated Sixteenth Battle of the Southern Hemisphere Aperture Stone, the Sund flew in to finish neutralizing and expel the invading Paralyzer. By this point, the Paralyzer's weapons were already sufficiently disabled, but its propulsion was not, so it required additional action from the thunclik fleet. For more information about the Battle of the Southern Hemisphere Aperture Stone, please read that entry.

Stormfish:

A variety of military airships ranging from lightweight fighter drone-carrying cruisers like the Silhouette, to heavy battleships like the Sund. For more specific information about the Silhouette or Sund, please read those entries.

Although the armaments vary among their airship categories, nearly all use gauss rail guns, some as rapid-fire turrets, some as artillery. In addition to the momentum negation technology, they also transfer momentum using six blocks of dense lead suspended by cables in rooms dedicated to their placement. Depending on the size of the airship, additional blocks may be needed, always in multiples of four. Their levitation is achieved using groups of subdivided atmospheric gas bladders with cells of heating coils and VTOL propulsors. These collect static electricity charges from the atmosphere by using a combination of the body's shape, the ramjet mouth intake, and the triboelectric effect of the "sweaters." This electric charge is created every time they move through the air, then channeled through a conductive wired network to batteries storing the voltage. The "sweaters" are gradually thickening layers of negatively charged hairlike fibers which "grab" atmospheric positive charges. These fibers connect with DC converters to ensure the safer voltage. When the hot-air bladders aren't in use, the excessive heat of the DC voltage is dispersed using heat fins immersed in coolant tanks. The captured electrical potential is dispersed back into atmosphere through the railguns.

Excessive charges are also dispersed back into the atmosphere with ionization grids in the aft of the stormfish. This is especially critical to reduce surface charges when docking. Although thunclik may be termed as creatures made of "living metal," stormfish are *not* "living ships," as this would require more than electrical energy. Some parts of these airships are made of "living metal" however and consequently require occasional replenishment for the same reasons thunclik do.

Svarsl:

Created from skjmyol milk, like a yogurt in consistency, this food looks, smells, and tastes like black coffee. Some varieties may be fermented, producing a "nose-tickling" alcoholic fizz. The preferences for svarsl are widely diverse—aged or fresh, taken with or without honey, numerous flavor additives, with a whole sub-industry and aficionados striving for the perfect cup of svarsl.

Svartfjella Aperture (Shifting Stones):

The Shifting Stones' side is located on the Southern Hemisphere Aperture Stone, while the other side is hidden in the Svartfjella Mountain Range. For more information about the Svartfjella Mountain Range, please read that entry. To protect the security and safety of the Shifting Stones, it is hidden by a combination of subtle means, both physical and psychological. Like all of the Shifting

Stones' Apertures, its exact location on Aerth is intended to be obscure, even in this story.

Svartfjella Mountain Range:

A line of mountains comprising part of the larger Jokudd Osst region belonging to the Vorth Union. A harshly cold environment in Aerth's subantarctic latitudes, most flora and fauna here is similar to Earth's tundra. Surrounding forests of blackcone pines defy the biting cold, though the trees will grow gnarled and bent to the wind by themselves.

Synchronized Perception and Integration Relay:

An interface for thunclik to connect their minds' decision-making abilities directly to local intranets for instantaneous reaction time with complex systems such as stormfish defense or flight maneuvers. It is through this interface that thunclik equipment is used as a literal extension of their bodies. This connection may occur through brainwave-sensing caps and VR goggles/gloves. or sometimes more directly with a fiber-optic cable. This allows thunclik to use their equipment as if it is a part of their body because temporarily, it is. The connection also allows them to share goals and intentions among the groups, applying a "hive mind" effect while choosing what to share, connecting or disconnecting as needed, and preserving private individuality.

Tasdo:

One of the five mortal races of Aerth, they are similar in day-to-day life and physical ability to anthropomorphic snakes. This inspiration is also reflected in some aspects of their cultural traditions. Physically, they are rather similar to the "nagas" depicted in Earth fantasy stories, a humanoid torso that moves around on a large snake tail as wide as the torso. For comparison, Earth's fantasy nagas mostly look completely human from the waist up, with a tail below. A Tasdo's torso is completely covered in scales and serpentine in other details of appearance. Though not truly warm-blooded in metabolism, they generate internal warmth through biological methane production ignited in specially contained organs for transmitting the heat. Contrary to how this sounds, Tasdo generally do *not* "breathe fire" like dragons. This would be too dangerous for their throats, mouths, and faces. Some Tasdo knife-tooth hosts have tried mutating this feature to project fire, with limited success.

The history of Tasdo cultures is replete with uncannily successful predictions of merchant trade. Whether in selecting optimal locations for trade routes, or dealing with previously unknown products, Tasdo are usually the best at business, though the other races have their own exceptional merchants. This encourages an excellent logic for courtroom procedures, and governmental and judicial decisions, encouraging many to become lawyers or similar specialists. Some Tasdo are able to apply this type of logic to learning about the sciences in biology or other areas that handle vast amounts of information. At least a quarter of the students at Aerth's prominent university, the Icadion, are typically Tasdo. A common trait for Tasdo intellectuals is an introverted personality.

Teleportation Pad Network:

A vital point-to-point teleportation network only accessible for thunclik needing to respond quickly to emergencies or hostile actions harming the Shifting Stones.

Thunclik:

A race of creatures serving the direct interests of Oruaural, and indirectly, the higher authority of Ekallr. Their bodies have features seamlessly meshing biological complexity with solid mechanical parts, even with interchangeable parts. One of the features combining organic form with mechanical parts is the thunclik's Stirling engine. In principle and form, it is an inorganic machine. The engine is connected with an electrical generator, which sends voltages throughout the thunclik's shape memory muscles. The ashes left from burned fuel are dissolved into the mercury bloodstream, distributing it throughout the body. The ashes' molecular bonds are stripped of all their metallic elements, then the nonmetallic remains are passed out through the skin. In addition to vocal speech, thunclik are also able to communicate over long-distance with radio transmissions similar in concept to telepathy, or via the shared data of the COBWEB computer network. For details about the COBWEB, please read that entry.

The combination of organic and mechanical forms in their metallic bodies allows thunclik to disconnect their torsos from their arachnid legs. The arachnid chassis of these may then be remotely operated by the torso, while the thunclik operates his or her torso through stored energy. This separation operation cannot work indefinitely, as the torso's energy is usually charged by the chassis' engine. Also, the thunclik derives physical replenishment from any remaining metallic elements left over from his or her engine's fuel consumption.

A fundamental basis of thunclik biology, is a distribution and absorption network for their engines' consumed fuel, even for those parts of a thunclik body that seem like mere solid metal, such as their titanium-beryllium bones or outer armor plating. To facilitate their metallic biology, the microscopic cells of a thunclik utilize molecular sequencing chain for their "DNA." However, this chain is completely different from carbon-based life, as a thunclik's "DNA" is a combination of different metallic base molecules in sequence.

The bases for these chains stick out from the center length like the vertebrae of a spine, arranged like the beads on a compacted string, insulated against an errant crossing connection with one-sided molecular bonds. As a whole, these metallic polymers are compacted into a molecular chain sequence. Though they are the "DNA" of a thun-clik, these chain sequences don't form X-shaped chromosomes, but carefully fold themselves into condensed cubes. These cubes of the metallic polymer chains—each a single chain—are the thunclik's "genes," which stack neatly on top of each other. The pattern replication is preserved by the chain passing through a molecular ring that "reads" the chain and draws in molecules to form new chain bases. New chains are moved into one half of the cell, which then prepares for cellular division.

Despite how some features seem apparently artificial, thunclik bodies grow to their full size in metallic "eggs" or "cocoons". For this reason, no young thunclik ever grows from a child's size to an adult. For this reason, thunclik bodies do not age like mortals do. With bodies made of metal, they may only suffer mild corrosion. When thunclik age, the only sign of this is a slowly increasing difficulty to make decisions and tarnished skin. This eventually requires reintegration with the COBWEB to refresh the data. If a thunclik's personality core is destroyed, his or her memory is used to create a replacement personality core through the COBWEB.

Although most thunclik are about the comparative size of an easy chair, there is some considerable variation of size depending on the specific tasks that individual thun-clik may be needed for. This developmental change to the thunclik's body may only be applied before he or she has hatched. The largest thunclik specialists are used in construction and are about the size of the average heavy industrial bucket loader. The Shifting Stones' library, the Skapgeh, is staffed by both mortals and thunclik serving Oruaural. The thunclik shelvers of this library are approximately two feet tall and behave and move like jumping spiders. They have similar personalities to the average human seven year old, with all of the referential knowledge and analytical ability of a supercomputer.

There are thousands of variations of thunclik specialist functionary needs. Technically, the bodies of airships like the stormfish could also count as a thunclik bodies because of how thoroughly the mind-to-machine interface is completed. But the individuals connecting this way are able to easily engage and disengage with VR goggles/gloves. Also, a stormfish's airship body is too large to be grown in an egg or cocoon. In special circumstances, thunclik airships may be fitted with personality cores but once integrated with the ship, the core cannot be removed without destroying it. For more information about stormfish, please read that entry.

Thvenel:

One of the five mortal races of Aerth, they are similar in day-to-day life and physical ability to giant hornets. This inspiration is also reflected in some aspects of their cultural traditions. Physically, they are lightweight, with wiry muscles strong enough to lift heavier loads than Vungir, but they have poorer stamina. Generally, most Thvenel are more aggressive than the mortal races, but work to restrain these traits, mostly in recognition of peace being more comfortable for everyone involved, but always ready to defend against the first who would attack. This encouraged a "noble warrior" type culture among the unconquered Thvenel kingdoms. The Grefarn however, encourage unrestricted aggression if it serves their political interests.

With a preference for building their structures from mixtures of clay, paper, and wood, Thvenel only build near forests. This encourages an industry in logging, carpentry, or other careers that work with the aforementioned materials. Unfortunately for many Thvenel, the recent "transformative" ideals of the new Grefarn Empire have thrown much of this into limbo. The Thvenel countries not under Grefarn control are benefiting greatly from their ability to meet customer demand, only because the Empire can't control them yet. Because of this, the remaining Thvenel kingdoms generally believe the Grefarn operate their tyranny under a philosophy of unrecognized stagnation and devastation. Unrecognized, but still sought after on a subtle level.

Veil:

Ernest's hometown, on the north side of the river separating it from Boston.

Vorth Union:

One of several dominant countries in Aerth. Both Hahn Stend-Stein and Laeljah Svartvaengra are citizens. Formerly, the Vorth Union pursued a mercantile trade with the Grefarn Empire but are now engaged in a Cold War with each other. The political situation in both countries is being stoked to unrest, as each side accuses their political enemies of manipulation, Vorth Union versus Grefarn Empire. Built upon the mutual desire that personal freedom can only exist if the source stems from a model of Ekallr's morality, because all societies have both good and bad people in them. A society that allows for the possibility of criminals to rule, will allow its foundation to be remade into whatever the criminals want. For a society to resist internal corruption, it must have an externalized moral authority that cannot be corrupted. With a 500-year-old history of seeking agreement after diverse discussion, allowing both majorities and minorities to speak, many Vorth citizens are proud of their heritage.

Vungir:

One of the five mortal races of Aerth, they are similar in day-to-day life and physical ability to bats. This inspiration is also reflected in some aspects of their cultural traditions. Physically, they have stout muscles for flying through the stormy weather that often sweeps over the mountainous regions they call home. Much like bats, Vungir are nocturnal, active at night, sleeping during the day, and also use sonar. Since they prefer building their homes underground to avoid the frequent blizzards, they usually look for natural caves, or excavate out of mountains or whatever ground will not be flooded.

This encourages a natural talent for mining, though these are not the cramped series of tunnels usually thought of with mining. Most Vungir cities have cavernous chambers dedicated first to their places of religious worship. Arranged in layered levels stacked like skyscraper floors, these pigeonhole apartments or businesses surround the aforementioned sanctums. This is purposed around the idea that if citizens are reminded of their faith every time they pass through the center of their community, it reminds them that good morality is the foundation of their society.

Whelming Smoke:

A smoke with an emotionally overpowering effect on anyone who breathes it in, causing them to feel intense fear and sadness. Even with a filtering mask, a victim suffering from an attack using this smoke may still be affected in a more limited way by the absorption of the substance through the skin. Whatever the dosage, the victim will find themselves focusing on their failures and any other disappointments of their past, thus overwhelming their thoughts. Since this effect is intensified by the normal senses of fear and sadness, the intensification may continue in a feedback loop. To interrupt the smoke's effect, the victim must concentrate on happier feelings, to force themselves to ignore their fears and failures. A good way to fight against the whelming smoke is to concentrate on rousing feelings, and to focus on faith and confidence. This interrupts the "feedback loop" intensification, allowing the victim a greater control to ignore the negative feelings, but this requires a strong faith. Any focus on the negative emotions, and they surge back again.

Yukar:

A foul expletive and curse. Common on the western coastline of the Fahiik continent.

CPSIA information can be obtained
at www.ICGtesting.com
Printed in the USA
LVHW051732011121
702142LV00004B/232

9 781662 831713